THE TOFF AND THE DEEP BLUE SEA

As the Honourable Richard Rollison, alias the Toff,
strolled along the promenade at Nice the women eyed
him with a longing that most men would have found
embarrassing. The reason for the looks was not, as
might have been supposed, his natural charm. No,
their interest was due to the fact that he was on the
Riviera engaging girls for M. Rambeau's new cabaret at
the *Baccarat*.

But an attempt on his life suggests that someone
knows that the real reason for his presence is to track
down a poor-little-rich-girl who's gone missing.

All lines of enquiry lead to the elusive Chicot, the
master. Chicot who, like his predecessor created by
Alexandre Dumas, may be a clown but is certainly no
fool.

THE TOFF AND THE DEEP BLUE SEA

John Creasey

·BLACK·
DAGGER
·CRIME·

First published 1955
by
Hodder & Stoughton Ltd
This edition 1990 by Chivers Press
published by arrangement with
the author's estate

ISBN 0 86220 785 1

Foreword copyright © John Kennedy Melling 1990

British Library Cataloguing in Publication Data available

*The characters in this book are entirely
imaginary and have no relation to any
living person*

Printed and bound in Great Britain by
Redwood Press Limited, Melksham, Wiltshire

FOREWORD

John Creasey was the founder of the Crime Writers' Association, and the author of more than six hundred books on crime and detection under seventeen *noms de plumes*—but not before he had received seven hundred rejection slips!

His character the Toff, the Honourable Richard Rollison, with monocle, impeccable dress, West End flat, and man Jolly, first appeared in *Thriller* Magazine in 1933, right at the start of Creasey's career, appearing in book form five years later. The Toff was essentially in the 1930s' tradition of what the Americans have termed 'silly assery'—examples of which include Campion, Wimsey, the Saint, etc, all elegant young men with money and the crusading spirit of a modern Robin Hood.

The present book first appeared in 1955, and the title is cleverly ambiguous. Betwixt the devil and the deep blue sea is a nautical term, with no relation to Satan, but to part of the hull of a ship. Finally the action of the story does indeed take place on the blue waters of the Mediterranean, chases, fights with Arab assassins, and lengthy enervating swims to shore.

Rollison goes to Nice, staying at the de luxe San Roman Hotel, which sounds like the Negresco or the now-vanished Ruhl, the changes at Nice having been many these last few years, with even Casinos closing. He is posing as the agent of the night club supremo Rambeau as he tries to discover the fate of various beautiful young girls, lured into a life of crime and confidence tricks, before vanishing—possibly into the white slave traffic. The master criminal is nicknamed Chicot, after the Dumas character, and his gang is well equipped with cars, yachts, and villas with secret passages—all so well done that the reader may well wonder how the Toff will again vanquish singlehanded, save for just two helpers.

Violent deaths occur, both to criminals and to Rollison's aides, and there are some well-drawn characters, like the immensely tall clown, Simon Leclair, whose presence on the Promenade des Anglais would cause no surprise since Nice is a favourite venue for French circuses; we once saw the legendary Achille Zsvatta performing there.

Some of Creasey's books are police procedurals, although he never claimed to be completely omniscient on police matters. Indeed, in this present book he explains in a note that he is not sure of the difference between the French *gendarmes* and the *agents de police*—not surprising when you recall there are five separate police forces in France. Others, like *The Toff and the Deep Blue Sea* are of a mystery type, with the master criminal unmasked at the dénouement in the final pages.

You are always sure of a rattling good story from John Creasey, one that carries you, with no let-up, from beginning to end. *The Toff and the Deep Blue Sea* is no exception, and it has the added bonus of giving the reader the incentive to visit the delightful town of Nice, a place with more *belle epoque* buildings than any city in France, save Paris.

JOHN KENNEDY MELLING

John Kennedy Melling, Black Dagger Editor, is no stranger to the Cote d'Azur, frequently appearing on Tele-Monte-Carlo, where on one occasion he was taken on the unprotected roof of the Transmitter at La Torbie to see the lights of Monte Carlo—a sheer drop of a mile below!

THE BLACK DAGGER CRIME SERIES

The Black Dagger Crime series is a result of a joint effort between Chivers Press and a sub-committee of the Crime Writers' Association, consisting of Marian Babson, Peter Chambers and chaired by John Kennedy Melling. It is designed to select outstanding examples of every type of detective story, so that enthusiasts will have the opportunity to read once more classics that have been scarce for years, while at the same time introducing them to a new generation who have not previously had the chance to enjoy them.

CONTENTS

I shall be grateful if the critical reader will forgive me, in these pages, for having used the word *gendarme* both in its proper sense and also in the place of *agent de police*. To tell the truth, I've never been able to distinguish one from the other.

J. C.

THE TOFF AND
THE DEEP BLUE SEA

1

A FRIEND FOR THE TOFF

THE Honourable Richard Rollison was walking along the promenade at Nice.

He was alone.

It was crystal clear that there was no need for him to be alone. Many gazed upon him, some with such obvious longing that most men would have found it embarrassing. He did not. Nor did he revel; instead, he rode through, as it were, not wholly oblivious but not deeply concerned. In fact, it was rather pleasant. Especially opposite the Hotel St. Germain, where the girl with the monstrous wide hat and the most seductive little figure on the Riviera, gazed longingly at him.

She nearly spoke.

He glanced at her, inclined his head with a gravity and a courtliness which would not have shamed a Frenchman of a century ago, and passed her by. She watched him go.

It was equally pleasant by the little shelter opposite the Hotel San Roman. The girl here was taller, built on a somewhat more generous scale, beautifully dressed, magnificently glamorous, and with hair so black that a raven would have looked upon it with envy.

She took a quick, timorous step forward.

Rollinson glanced at her also, and inclined his head in the grand manner, and walked by; she watched him tensely, if not tearfully, as if every thought in her mind were urging her to follow but some fear held her back.

The promenade at Nice is wide, spacious, and free to all. It may cost a fortune to have a room with a balcony overlooking the breath-taking beauty of the headland to the left, and the sea which is as shimmering and as blue as imagination ever suggested; but it costs nothing to walk along the promenade. It may cost a beggar a day's food and lodgings to have a drink on the terrace of the Hotel San Roman, but it costs nothing to stand outside and watch the orchestra and listen to the music.

It is also a good place to beg, if one has cunning.

The *gendarmes*, with their little white batons and dark-blue uniform and truculent manner, will drive away all importunate beggars—those ill-advised enough to ask for alms—but they can do nothing with the beggar who simply stands near by, or crouches, and watches one with pleading eyes.

Several such beggars were on the promenade that morning, and they saw the Englishman with the perfectly cut grey suit, the virgin white shoes, the subdued and yet noticeable tie, the dark hair, and the good looks. He made quite a picture to behold. Connoisseurs would probably have agreed that no better-dressed man had walked the promenade that season. But none, least of all the beggars, believed that the way the beautiful girls looked upon him was a tribute to his looks.

That would have been shameless.

Whatever yearning burned in the hearts and minds of those who watched him pass, it was not for a soul-mate or a lover. The yearning was very, very different.

Rollison reached a spot on the promenade which was not lined, as it were, with such feminine delectability. In fact, it seemed deserted. He moved towards the rail, and leaned upon it. He looked down at the large pebbles of the beach and the lapping water, running gently to and fro among the pebbles. He looked upon the gaily striped umbrellas, offering shade from the warm sun. He watched children swimming. He saw one man fifty yards out, breaking the glass-like surface of the sea with long, powerful strokes; his arms and shoulders were tanned mahogany brown. The swimmer was a sight to see, yet Rollison did not watch for him; instead, he allowed his gaze to travel.

Not far off two young women lay on their faces, their backs completely bare, a trifling piece of red about the nether regions of one and blue on those of the other, saving them from absolute nudity. Their skin was golden brown. One moved, slowly, wriggling a lovely shoulder, and then her arms moved and her hands clutched at unseen things. She fiddled, and then lay still. She had fastened the top of her *bikini*, and now, without shame, was able to sit up, to yawn, and then to lie down on her back and roast her fair skin on the other side.

The Englishman watched.

A beggar stood by.

The sun grew hotter.

The yearning lovelies watched, too.

Then a couple passed, leaving Rollison and the beggar together; they were out of earshot of anyone else. Rollison put a hand in his pocket and brought out money, as if to give alms, and smiled amiably and asked in fluent French:

"Is she here?"

"No, *m'sieu.*"

"Sure?"

"I have walked the whole promenade, *m'sieu,* from one end to the other, and she is not here. Five times I have done that." Beautiful brown eyes, velvety and sad, looked into the grey eyes of the Englishman, not at the hand which held the *mille francs* notes. The beggar wore only a shirt, which was darned, trousers, which were patched, and brown shoes, which badly needed mending. His pale-brown hair was long and peppered with grey. He was one of nature's ugly men, but the beauty of his eyes made it easy to forget that.

"Keep looking," urged Rollison, and placed two of the notes into a hand which was surprisingly clean for one of nature's less fortunate children. He smiled again, and turned away as the beggar uttered his thanks in a quiet voice.

The beggar also turned away.

Rollison walked back, at the same slow pace, towards the great hotels, the people lazing on terraces and balconies, the bathers, the sun-worshippers, the people sitting on deck-chairs on the promenade. A very fat woman wearing a tweed coat, a shapeless tweed skirt, and a little man's cap, looked as red as any beetroot as she moved among the deck-chairs. She was collecting her ten francs from those who sat on canvas, giving a ticket in exchange, and going on to the next.

She looked like an artist's impression of Madame Guillotine herself.

On the right, the sea; lovely enough to hurt.

On the left, the road, the line of exotic palm-trees down the middle, and on the other side, the great hotels, mostly painted white or cream, some pale blue or yellow, pink or green. There was some traffic. Bright new Renaud and Citroen taxis; here and there, a decrepit old cab, almost shamed to show its bonnet in the midst of such brash plenitude. Bright new American cars, with shade-giving vizors, gave a hint of opulence. Gleaming new British cars were of fabulous value. Colourful *fiacres* with gay canopy shades were drawn by horses which trotted briskly and guided, if guided were the word, by old men who seemed to be dozing in the morning warmth. Here was Nice in all its picture-postcard beauty, redeeming every promise it had ever made about the weather; adorned with those beautiful women, too.

Into all this, lolloped a clown.

He was driving a ridiculously little car, bright red and almost fresh from the conveyor belts of the great Renault factory on the island in the Seine. He looked much too big for this automobile. The roof, which rolled back like a wooden shop-front, was wide open, showing the clown's head. He was bald on top, but around the bald patch flaming red hair was thick and bushy, and blown by the wind which the movement of the car created. He had a long nose. He had wrinkled eyelids, and these drooped so much that it was possible to believe that he was dozing at the wheel, thus accounting for the fact that he was doing no more than twenty kilometres an hour. Impatient and opulent British and American cars hooted and surged past him. An old man, sitting erect behind a dapple grey horse, flicked his whip, made his horse canter, and threatened to overtake the tiny car.

Then the car swung into the kerb, and stopped. Brakes squealed. The driver of the *fiacre* cursed magnificently. People stared.

All this was near the Hotel San Roman, and the dark-haired girl who had nearly followed Rollison. Rollison was on a level with her again, and but for the squeal of brakes she would almost certainly have stopped in front of him.

He turned.

She stared.

The little car jolted to a standstill, its single door opened, its clown-like driver uncoiled himself. He had to bend almost double in order to get out. Once on the pavement, he straightened up, as a spring might; sight and movement were unbelievable; one waited for the creaking of joints. And one remembered ridiculous clowns with enormous trousers and elongated boots, check shirts and silly hats, who climbed out of toy automobiles and squirted water into the faces of others who rushed to the rescue.

This clown needed no rescuing. He ran towards Rollison. Running, he was a sight to see, for his long legs had very bony knees which seemed to be thrusting their way through the cloth of his trousers. His arms waved, like a child's out of control. His elbow threatened everyone who drew near. He had a fantastically ugly face and a huge mouth, which was wide open as he cried:

"*M. le Toff! M'sieu! M. le Toff!*"

The word 'toff', familiar to English ears and on an English tongue, sounded strange from a Frenchman. But none who watched—including the beauty with the generous curves and the timidity—was concerned with what he said, but how he said it. His voice travelled far, and must surely have been heard by the man who was still cleaving the calm water with his sun-browned arms and legs; and it was probably heard high up in the hotels, as far away as those rooms which cost only half a fortune because they had no balcony—only a window with a view.

"*M. le Toff!*" roared the clown, although now he was only a few feet away from Rollison; and it was clear that Rollison was the object of his attentions. That was not surprising, since 'Toff' had been his soubriquet for twice as many years as he cared to remember.

Rollison didn't speak, but beamed almost as widely as the clown, and held out both his hands in welcome. The clown, long lean body, arms and legs waving in a kind of perpetual motion, ignored his hands and flung his arms round Rollison's shoulders, and hugged him as a mistress would hug a long-lost lover. Then he held Rollison by the shoulders, thrust him back as if to make sure that no feature of the handsome face was missing, and then, with the greatest deliberation any man was capable of, he kissed him roundly on either cheek.

"George!" a girl exclaimed in the English of Hackney, "look at *that*."

"Hush, it's none of our business." An embarrassed young Englishman hustled his lady love away.

Salutation over, the clown released the Toff, and stood grinning down upon him. This in itself was remarkable, for the Toff was six-feet one. To see the top of his old friend's head, he had to stand some distance off, for there was six feet eight inches of Simon Leclair.

"Well, well," he said in English, "you grow taller and thinner, but you're losing your hair. Simon, this is wonderful!"

"*Won*-derful!" boomed Simon Leclair, with accented English of great clarity, "superb, magnificent, what the doctor ordered. How are you?"

"Fine."

"*Bewt*-iful!" cried Leclair. "My friend, we have the

drink. Come." Suddenly, he looked alarmed, and past the Toff towards the dark-haired lovely. "You are not alone, yes?"

"Alone."

"*Alone?*" echoed Simon unbelievingly. "No one is with you?"

"No one is with me."

"No lady?"

"No lady."

"Toff," began Simon Leclair, lowering his voice as one might in a sickroom, "you are not so well?"

Rollison chuckled, and turned towards the road. They had to cross it in order to reach the San Roman, where he was staying, and the terrace where music was being played now. This music came softly and remotely, for those who had been at the casino until the small hours were not yet awake; and these were mostly wealthy clients who had to be given the utmost consideration.

"I'm fine," said Rollison. "How's Fifi?"

"Fifi," echoed Simon, and gurgled and clapped his great hands. "How happy Fifi will be to see you."

"Is she here, too?"

"But of course, friend Toff. Can you imagine Fifi permitting me to come to Nice on my own?" Laughter shook the clown's body, seeming to rumble up and down his long, pipe of a neck. "Oh, what a good one that is! No, sir, she comes to look after me; we are both in the act."

"Ah," said Rollison, and there was a slight change in the tone of his voice and in the way he looked. "What act is it this time, Simon?"

"Where else would it be but the *Baccarat*?" asked Simon Leclair, flinging his huge red hands about and ending up with one upon the Toff's shoulder. "The best show in Nice, isn't it? In *Nice*?" He roared with laughter. "In the whole of the Riviera, in the whole of France, in the whole——"

Then a strange and frightening thing happened.

A car, travelling fast, swung off the road towards the Toff and Simon Leclair, making the beautiful woman with the raven-black hair cry out in sudden fear.

Her fears were for the Toff.

2

THE QUESTIONS OF SIMON

THE Toff saw the car coming.

He saw other things, too. At the wheel was a pleasant-looking young man in a navy-blue reefer jacket, wearing a silk scarf, his dark hair brushed smoothly back from a pale forehead. By the young man's side was a girl, a blonde—and she was terrified.

The car was a big Citroen, and had been travelling at fully sixty kilometres, which was illegal and nearly murderous. When the Toff first saw it swing towards him off the road, it was only a few yards away.

"*Nom d'un nom*," breathed Simon Leclair in a quivering whisper, for he was in equal danger. He pushed at the Toff, but the Toff was already jumping out of the way. Simon flung himself in the other direction. The wings of the car passed within inches of them both as they fell—much as the sea is cleft by the sharp bows of a ship. The engine stalled. The car stopped. The black-haired girl on the promenade was staring at the Toff, her gloved hand at her mouth. She was biting on to her hand; not pretending, biting.

The Toff knew that he was on the ground, and unhurt; at least, not seriously hurt. He did not pick himself up, but groaned, and then moved his body, as if in agony; but actually he moved so that he was facing the driver of the big

Citroen. He looked at the back of the man from beneath his long lashes.

People bent over the Toff. . . .

For a split second the driver of the killer car sat at the wheel, as if shocked to immobility. But he wasn't. The Toff had caught a glimpse of his expression as the car had hurtled at them. There had been no look of dread, as on the girl's; no horror, as there would surely be on the face of a man who had lost control of a car and was likely to kill or to maim.

He had known what he was about; which meant that the affair had been no accident.

At last the driver relaxed and moved; the blonde girl by his side began to shiver; a little man with waxed moustaches and a beard fifty years out of fashion turned towards the handsome young driver and, shaking both fists, hurled a bewildering selection of accusations at him, not the least offensive of which was *imbécile*.

Policemen came running.

Quite a crowd gathered round Rollison, all agog for blood. He lay with his eyes flickering and his lips tightening as if in pain. Hands touched him, men shouted orders—to lift him, to leave him there, to turn him on his back, to straighten his legs, to move his arms, to give him air, to give him water; advice flew hither and thither in great debate. Rollison, convinced that the young man had known what he was doing, wanted to feign injury, but he was desperately anxious about Simon.

That anxiety was dispersed in a flash. He heard Simon's deep voice—it was very deep for a Frenchman—delivering a prodigious variety of epithets at the Citroen's youthful driver. Through his lashes, Rollison saw the red hair and the bald patch; there was nothing at all to worry about—except perhaps the girl with the beautiful black hair. She was on the fringe of the crowd, and something of her terror still showed in her eyes.

Those eyes reminded Rollison of the beggar's.

"*Voici M. le médecin!*" an excitable little man cried out, and Rollison submitted himself to the ministrations of a doctor. . . .

Simon gave unstinted unprofessional advice.

Rollison was poked, prodded, and moved gently; then he let it be known that he was coming round. Whenever anyone touched his left leg, he winced or groaned. He was given a sip of water, then some brandy, next a whiff of smelling-salts—which did in fact do much to clear his head; the only bruise he had was just above his left temple.

He grunted, opened his eyes as if bewilderedly, listened to this gabble of comment, saw that Simon was positively pinning the youthful driver with the sleek black hair against the trunk of a phœnix pine, holding him there with one long fore-finger and gesticulating generously with his free right hand. A *gendarme* was aiding and abetting. The girl sat in her seat, her eyes closed. The beggar found a way through the crowd, looking very hard at Rollison, and for the first time Rollison tried to convey a message.

The difficulty was to know what message, for he was as eager to know more of the Citroen driver as about the black-haired girl. But the police would surely take the driver's name and address, whereas the girl might vanish.

So Rollison looked from the beggar to the girl with the black hair and brown eyes.

The beggar followed the direction of his gaze, and with a nod that was almost imperceptible, he turned away. By then, willing hands were helping Rollison to his feet. He stood on one leg, leaning against a burly porter from the San Roman.

The beggar now stood near the raven-haired girl.

"*M'sieu* must have rest," pleaded the porter, who knew this Englishman as a most generous client. "If you please, *M. le médecin*, M. Rollison must have rest."

It was most confusing for the next five minutes. Finally, a kind of canvas sling chair, used for helping the helpless in and out of cars, was brought into service. Rollison was loaded on to it, and the *gendarmes* hurried, with their batons raised, to form a kind of guard of honour across the road. By then the crowd had swollen from dozens to many hundreds. The orchestra outside the San Roman was playing to almost deserted terraces, and would have no love for the cause of such desertion.

Simon stayed away from the hotel.

The doctor accompanied Rollison and the porters carrying him. The raven-haired girl stayed on the promenade, the beggar nearby.

In the hotel it was cool.

Upstairs in Rollison's bedroom it was pleasant, too. The room had a balcony overlooking the bay, and the tree-clad hills which fell into the sea, all dotted with white villas. The coloured awning was down, to shut out the sun. A chambermaid was already on duty, turning down the bed, most eager to help. Rollison was stripped of his coat and of his trousers. The doctor prodded at his knee, and Rollison winced. He also gave a long-suffering look, although it did not hurt at all. The doctor prescribed bathing with a lead lotion, and then a tight bandage, gave precise instructions, and went out with the porter and the under-manager, who had tagged along from downstairs. So Rollison was alone, except for the maid.

She was a pretty little thing, also possessed of brown eyes and dark hair. She was a little timid, too, for she came from one of the vine-valleys of Bordeaux, and did not know or greatly like the ways of some of the wealthy patrons of the San Roman. Some pinched, kissed or poked, none of which was nice, but this Englishman . . .

"Suzanne," said the Toff.

"*M'sieu?*"

"Do you think you could bring me some tea?"

"At once, *m'sieu!*" She beamed her desire to serve, then hurried out.

The moment the door was closed, Rollison got up and used his left leg as if he had been practising for the long jump or the hurdles. He sped to the door, turned the key in the lock, moved round, and stepped cautiously on to the balcony.

Here, in spite of the shade, it was much warmer.

By keeping to one side, Rollison could make sure that he wasn't seen, even if anyone looked up, and there seemed little likelihood of that. The crowd remained. Simon, standing in the shadow of the phœnix palm, was talking and moving his arms and legs about like pistons; one second his red hair looked like flame in the sun, the next it was dulled as he moved into shadow.

The youthful driver, freed from the pinioning finger, was now besieged by *gendarmes*, one of whom was making notes. The raven-haired girl was walking away, and the beggar following her; in fact, had it not been for the beggar, Rollison could not have been sure that it was the same girl.

The killer car's driver did not once look at the blonde who had been sitting with him, and was still in her place. She looked nice, mused Rollison; he wished that there was a way to have her followed and so find out more about her; but if he was to keep up the legend of his injured knee and consequent incapacity, he couldn't do a thing.

Well, the police would have that name and address.

Simon moved from the crowd, and crossed the road, and Suzanne arrived with the tea.

She should not have done, for that was a waiter's privilege, but the San Roman also had its staffing problems, and a willing girl was ever welcome.

When she came in, the door had been unlocked and Rollison was back in bed. Before she left, there was a tap at the door.

"See who it is, will you?" asked Rollison, although he felt quite sure that it would be Simon.

It was a bell-boy, a curly-haired imp of mischief in wine-red uniform, a tight-fitting jacket, bright silver buttons, and a silver salver. Suzanne took the letter on the salver, shooed the boy away, and brought the letter to the Toff. Scrawled

on it in faint pencilled writing was his name: *M. Rollison.*
It was sealed, and at the back was the embossed crest of the
San Roman.

"All right, Suzanne," said Rollison, and smiled. "Leave
the door so that anyone can come in, will you, please?"

"Of course, m'sieu."

Rollison wondered what was keeping Simon, and guessed
that the clown was involved in yet another argument. He also
wondered who had written to him, opened the letter, and
smoothed out a single sheet of the expensive San Roman
letter-heading, with the same expensive embossed monogram.

He read the pencilled words: *"Please, will you see me? I
call at your room at twelve o'clock."* There was no signature,
nothing except the sloping hand to tell him whether this was
a man or a woman's writing; and the slope did not indicate
either for certain. He poured himself tea, lit a cigarette, and
then heard footsteps outside. These were followed, a moment
later, by a loud thump at the door of his room.

"Come in, Simon!" he called.

This time Simon appeared, bending low so that he could
get into the room from the wide passage. Standing upright,
he was two inches taller than the lintel. The room, though
not over-large, had its own small bathroom, the door of
which was open. One of Simon's elbows vanished into the
bathroom as he came in and closed the passage door. Once
inside, he straightened up to his full height, and bumped his
head against one of two hanging chandeliers. Porcelain and
gilt rattled; he swore, ducked, rubbed his head and glared.

"There should be one only, and that in the middle!"

"Agreed," said Rollison politely. "Would you like a cup
of tea?"

Simon looked blank.

"Your pardon?"

"I was offering you a cup of tea."

"Tea," echoed Simon, and regarded the tray. He had huge
eyes, and the droop of the wrinkled lids was natural, not

even slightly due to affectation. But he could open them
wide, and did so now. They were a greeny-brown colour,
very fine and clear, and filled with the deep repugnance that
he felt.

"No," he said roundly. "I would not."

"There's a bottle of whisky in——"

"You must be hurt very badly," Simon declared. "You
offer me tea. You talk to me of whisky. The one blows out
my belly, and what do I have for *déjeuner, hein?* The second
burns me like the vitriolic acid. And this in *la belle France*,
where——"

"There is a spot of Belsac '45 in the wardrobe," murmured
Rollison apologetically.

"My friend," said Simon, with new, strange gentleness,
"your body may be broken, but your head is still very sound.
Thank you." He went to the wardrobe and had to go down
on his knees to get the bottle out; glasses were on the dressing
table. He poured the wine as if it were liquid gold, and
savoured and sipped as if it were the finest brandy from
Cognac. That done, he pulled up an arm-chair and sat down,
thrusting his long legs in front of him. He seemed a long way
off, although his feet were actually hidden beneath Rollison's
bed. "The man driver," he announced, "will have severe
punishment. He is an imbecile. I," declared Simon, with
great satisfaction, "told him some things or two."

Rollison grinned.

"For the girl with him, I feel sorry," went on Simon.
"For myself, I feel sorry. For you, I feel sorry. For the
driver, I would like to break his neck. What a thing to do!
Sixty kilometres an hour. Sixty! Criminal that he is. He
blames the dog, a little dog that goes pit-pat-pit across the
road." Simon moved the fingers of his right hand when he
said pit-pat-pit, and it was almost as if a little dog were
running. "*Six*ty kilometres. He should be put in prison
for——"

"There was no dog," announced Rollison.

"It was only a little dog. You understand," went on Simon, earnestly, and as if it had been a mistake to speak English, "*un petit chien*. Pit-pat-pit it went across the road, and the imbecile was travelling so fast that——"

"There was no pit-pat-pit," murmured Rollison, "because there was no dog."

"*Un petit chien*," pleaded Simon.

"*Non, mon ami, il n'y avait pas de petits chiens, de grands chiens, de chats, ou de souris.*"

"But it was just a little dog," begged Simon.

"That was the driver's excuse. He tried to run us down. Have you any enemies?" inquired the Toff earnestly.

"Have *I*?" breathed Simon. "Enemies? No, it is——" He stopped, licked his thick lips, and opened his huge eyes at their widest. Then he leaned forward. "*You* have the enemy. He tries to kill you."

"Kill or injure," compromised Rollison. "I'm afraid so."

"But—but, my friend, why?" asked Simon, in a faltering falsetto. "You are——" He stopped again, and the light of understanding dawned slowly in his eyes; it was remarkable that it had not shown before. "You mean, you are here on the business? The detection? *Sapristi*, what a fool I am not to know about that, of course! The detection! What, who, where, why, how——"

"I'll tell you," promised Rollison; "but before we go any further, do you know who the car driver is?"

"The first name, Raoul—the second I did not secure. He resides at the Villa Seblec——"

"Near here?"

"I do not know. I can find out if——"

"Wait a minute," interrupted the Toff urgently, and the clown stopped; and outside there sounded the clear sound of a big bell. "Isn't that twelve o'clock striking?" He listened, and the notes of a nearby clock became unmistakable. "Go and hide in the bathroom, will you? I'm expecting a visitor. Don't let her know you're there."

Very slowly, Simon uncoiled himself. Standing at his full height, he looked down upon the Toff from great, wide open eyes. Slowly, he closed one of them, and the resultant wink was the best-known wink in the whole of France. From the stage of the *Folies Bergère* to the most exclusive night-clubs of the Champs Elysées, it had made thousands upon thousands roar with laughter, for it was a wink which conveyed the meaning of all the winks in the world, and passed all language barriers.

"I begin to understand," he said hollowly. "I go. I shall return."

He stalked off, disappeared into the bathroom, and left the door ajar. There was no sound from him, no sound in the hotel. But the strains of a lilting tune travelled up from the orchestra, more vigorous now because it was after midday, and the slothful could be disturbed.

Someone was to come at twelve o'clock.

It was now three minutes past.

3

TALE OF A MISSING GIRL

IT was fifteen minutes past twelve. The orchestra below on the terrace was playing an air from *Guys and Dolls*, and it did not sound incongruous. Occasionally other sounds floated upwards: the scrape of chairs on the mosaic of the terrace, the chink of glasses, the hoot of horns, the clip-clop-clip-clop of the horses drawing the *fiacres*. The room was still deep in shadow, but through one chink in the awning Rollison could see the vivid light of the sky; outside it was really hot.

It was plenty warm enough in the room.

A woman approached the room, hurrying. Rollison sat up against his big, square pillow, the bedspread over his legs, a half-smoked cigarette between his thumb and forefinger. But the woman passed, and only the sounds from the orchestra floated into the room.

The bathroom door opened, and Simon's red nose and red hair and bald patch appeared, rather as if he were peering into the room from the ceiling.

"Stood up," he declared.

"Let down," said the Toff mournfully.

"May I come out of here now?"

"I think you'd better," said the Toff. As Leclair came into the room, he took the letter from the bedside table and held it out. "Man or woman, boy or girl?" he mused. "Whoever it was might have telephoned, unless prevented by forces beyond his or her control. Sit down, Simon, and be patient."

"Friend," said Simon, lowering himself into the chair, "you must have been very badly hurt. You are upset. The detective does not detect, no?"

"No."

"What," asked Simon earnestly, "does the detective look for?"

Rollison regarded him, long and lingeringly, and then said with great precision:

"A beautiful blonde."

"For beautiful blondes, you have only to crook your finger," Simon remarked. "If you do not believe me, there is Fifi as evidence. She may not be beautiful, but she is certainly a blonde, and whenever she sees you——"

"This one is English."

"You know her?"

"I've never seen her. It is not an affair of the heart," asserted the Toff. He was still cocking an ear in the hope that a sound would come from the passage, heralding the caller. "This is important but secret business," he went on. "I'm looking for a poor little rich girl who disappeared from her home three months ago. Her parents are frantic, not knowing where she is. She was known to have come to Nice, and to be with a man whose description is very vague. A wealthy man was swindled of a big sum of money, and there was plenty of evidence that this beautiful English blonde helped to make a fool of him. Her parents don't want to believe it, but it's true. That's the last that was heard of her. The police were asked to find her, and traced her to the *Baccarat*, where she sang for a few nights. Then—vanish."

"My friend," said Simon Leclair, with great earnestness, "you and I, we are grown men. We look the facts in the face. There are many pretty girls, blonde girls, dumb girls, who come to the Riviera for the gay life." Without a moment's warning, he flung up his hands, shrugged his shoulders to a swift, contagious rhythm, and emitted a saxophone solo from his rounded lips.

He stopped.

"They get into the hands of the rascals, and they ruin themselves," he went on. "What then? They are ashamed to go home to poppa and mama, so they stick around. Sad, but true. My Fifi could tell you a thing or two about girls who thought they would win fame or fortune here, and lost everything. When pretty bodies are taken out of the sea on the Côte d'Azur, my friend, the police do not embalm them and place them on the promenade for all to see. It is hush, hush, hush, and a very quiet funeral. Hush, hush, hush," repeated Simon sombrely, and moved the fingers of his right hand in a slow rhythm; as men in a cortège would move. "It is sad, it is life, it is death. And the father of this girl asks you to look where the police succeeded not?"

"Yes."

"I can understand that," remarked Simon. "In the desperation they want the amateur, and in these parlous days it is necessary for you to earn the odd penny, eh? Three-figure fee and all expenses paid, that's it?"

"Simon," murmured the Toff.

"Toff," murmured Simon.

"You're quite right. But I've met the mother and father of this pretty little blonde, and don't like to think of them unhappy as they are." Rollison could be impressively sincere. "She's their only child, and came late in their life. One of the tragedies. They spoiled, petted and fussed her, were more like grandparents than real parents. Then they woke up one day to find, to their horror, that she had gone. They believed she would come back. They prayed she would. They were ready to forgive anything. She didn't return. They tried every means to find her, and as a last resort, asked me to help. I'd like to."

He sounded as if he meant it; and he did.

"I also would like to," said Simon politely. "How are you trying, and what happened when you were nearly run down by the imbecile in that car?" Simon winced as he finished, and snapped his fingers with a noise like the pulling of a champagne cork. "*Sapristi!* Not an *imbécile*, a murderer!"

"The girl was known to be fascinated by the stage," said Rollison. "She once did a song-and-dance piece in a small dive in London. They guessed that she would be looking for a job like that here; that's how it was they traced her to the *Baccarat*. Have you ever heard of the great Rambeau, King of the Night Clubs?"

"Have I ever heard ——" began Simon, and drew his legs up so that his knees almost met his chin; he looked as if he were praying. "The famous impressario, whose *boîtes de nuit* is all the rage of London and New York. Who comes soon to the Riviera? Who is going to stage the biggest cabaret show in the whole of France? My friend, who has *not* heard of the great Rambeau? Why do you think that Leon, of the *Baccarat*, sends for the one and only Simon Leclair and his Fifi, *hein*? I tell you. Only the best is good enough to compete with the great Rambeau, so, we come. Why do you ask me if I have heard of Rambeau?"

"For the time being," said Rollison, "I am posing as Rambeau's agent. I am engaging the girls for his show, the artistes, everything. Rambeau," added Rollison, "is a good friend of mine. He agreed to let me represent him. So I've spread the word that I'm looking for girls for the greatest cabaret in France, and——"

"Hope this girl you seek will apply?" boomed Simon.

"Yes."

"And no?"

"She hasn't. A lot of girls have, though. There have been times when it's hardly been safe to go out alone," continued Rollison, smiling faintly. "I think I've seen every would-be leg-show all-show girl in Nice, Cannes, Menton, Monte Carlo, and a surprising lot of other places. I've seen them from the age of fifteen to four-score and fifteen. I swear one was nearer a hundred than ninety, yet still able to dance. I've seen hundreds upon hundreds, Simon, and the girl wasn't among them."

Simon considered all this, and then declared:

"It is sad, but you will never find her."

"I'm not so sure about that," said Rollison very softly. "I'm not at all sure, Simon Leclair. I've asked for her by name, just casually—I asked some of the girls if they'd ever met her, saying that if they had it would be worth their while to tell me. No one told me, but"—he tapped the letter—"I had this message—and someone tried to run me down. And I came across a beggar who says that he saw her near here, only last week."

"Last *week*?"

"That's right," said Rollison. "I don't say that I'd vouch for the beggar in a court of law, but he looks honest, and his eyes are always open for the main chance. He says that the girl whose photograph I showed him was at the far end of the promenade, alone, last week. He was there, he has a niche where he sleeps, and was going to it. The girl was frightened——"

"Frightened?" interjected Simon.

"Yes. He says that he asked her if he could be of any help, and she just stared at him, then burst into tears. Then a car drew up, a man jumped out, flung him a thousand francs, and told him the girl was having boy-friend trouble. This man drove the girl away." Rollison paused, then picked up another cigarette and lit it. "The beggar and I together have seen the three bodies which have been washed up this week within the boundaries of Nice, Cannes, and Monte Carlo. The girl wasn't among them."

"You pay this beggar?" asked Simon abruptly.

"A little."

"To a beggar, your little may be a fortune," said Simon wisely. "He might tell you all this so that you would keep on paying him. Let *me* deal with this beggar. I shall be able to tell you whether he is telling the truth."

"Later, perhaps," promised Rollison. "Simon, there were two girls this morning. I'd seen them both when they came for an audition. *Very* nice," he added, almost as an aside; and there was a reminiscent smile at his lips. "Very nice indeed; quite ready to show off their charms to Rambeau's agent, when their beauty of figure could speak for itself. They were on the promenade. They wanted to speak to me. They didn't because they dared not. I wish I knew why."

"Why do you think?" demanded Simon.

"You mean, what do I guess?" Rollison hesitated, and said firmly: "I think they're being watched. I think that one of them sent me the note saying she'd be here at twelve and stayed away because she was afraid to keep the appointment. Or else she was prevented. I don't like anything that's going on."

"But——" began the clown, and stopped.

"Yes?"

"The attempt to run you down suggests that you are beginning to learn," declared Simon, rubbing his great hands together and making a noise that was peculiarly his own; it could sound through a packed auditorium like distant thunder. "Is that what you think? That imbecile driver——"

"He's certainly a man to watch," agreed the Toff. "I wish I knew why he chose to run me down when he did, Simon. What do I know that scares him? Or what does he think I know?"

Simon said: "We have to find that out! What is there to do next?" His great eyes were open at their widest. "How can I help you? Who is this missing blonde?"

"There's a photograph of her in the top drawer," Rollison said.

Simon turned, stretched out a fabulously long arm, opened the drawer, and plucked out the photograph. He studied it, eyes narrowed, lids like shutters. The Toff could not see it, but knew it almost as well as he knew his own face.

The girl was Daphne Robina Myall. She was pretty and she had charm, but she was not really beautiful. There was more character than beauty in her face—one of the things which surprised the Toff, for usually girls who lost their heads and tried to make a fortune or else to find fame in the *demi-monde* of France were empty-headed floosies, sisters to the original dumb blonde. Daphne Myall was not empty-headed. He had checked everything her parents had told him with many others: with friends, with the headmistress of her expensive and exclusive school, with her dressmakers, her milliner, her hairdresser; and all were agreed that she was no fool.

And they said that whatever she wanted she was likely to get. She no more thought of taking no for an answer than she would have thought of entering a vow of silence. Like so many who had filled a pretty head with stardust, she longed for the fame of the footlights; and someone unknown had promised her that fame here.

Now she had vanished.

If the little old beggar with the fine brown eyes had not lied to Rollison, she had been here a week ago.

"What is it that we do next?" asked Simon Leclair, and so committed himself to the task. "You may be a badly injured man, but I am hale and hearty." To prove it, he thumped his chest with great vigour. "What can I do for you, my good friend? Today is Thursday. On Monday I begin at the *Baccarat*; until then I am free, Fifi is free, and we will do everything we can to help."

Rollison did not answer.

"My friend, there must be *some*thing we can do," insisted Simon, and looked as if he were about to burst into tears. His double-jointed body slumped into a position of utter dejection, his mobile face assumed an expression of deep gloom. As he had clowned his way to the top of his world, so he clowned his way through life, as if it were an act which never really finished. He looked at Rollison from beneath his lashes, then began to rock gently to and fro.

Rollison watched him thoughtfully.

"Something," pleaded Leclair. "Find this Raoul, find the Villa Seblac——"

"We can do that any time," said Rollison. "The question is, what's less obvious? The simple thing, I think. Find out who knows me here—who knows who I am and what I do. If it's generally known that I'm a private eye, it won't help at all, but if very few know it, we might be able to trace a line back. Will you do that?"

"Of course," promised Simon, and began the lengthy process of standing up, first looking askance at the chandeliers to make sure that he didn't bang his head. He was crouching when the telephone bell rang, and continued his upwards movement while watching Rollison lift the receiver and say ' 'Allo', a Frenchman to the life.

As he listened, his expression changed. He looked into Simon Leclair's eyes, and his own were cold and hard. It was only a few seconds, but it seemed an age before he said:

"Yes, someone will come, Gaston. Where did you say?"

He paused again, said: "Yes, I understand," twice, and

then rang off. Simon was now standing upright, his head only a few inches from the ceiling. He did not speak but waited hopefully and expectantly.

"That was my beggar," Rollison said softly. "He's seen the girl again, on a boat rounding the point at Cap Mirabeau. And I'm stuck *here*." He clenched his hands, gritted his teeth, and almost overdid it. "Simon, you've seen her picture; go and see if——"

"I am on my way," said Simon Leclair, and made a swift movement towards the door. "If she is there, I shall find her!" He slid out of the door and closed it noiselessly behind him.

As the latch clicked, Rollison pushed back the bedspread, jumped out of bed, and dressed with furious speed.

4

POOR LITTLE BEGGAR

SIMON believed that Rollison's leg was so badly injured that he must rest it. The manager believed it. Porters believed it. The sleek-haired driver of the car which had nearly run him down almost certainly believed it. That made a number of pertinent reasons why it would be wise for Rollison to continue to pretend that he was *hors de combat*. But he might step out of the room and bang into Suzanne, who could be squared; or into a waiter, who couldn't; and he might get away with the ruse for hours or even days. There was now an enemy, known to exist, if unknown in identity; and the more the unknown could be fooled, the better.

Rollison rang for Suzanne, then bent down, opened the bottom drawer of the ornate dressing-table, and took out a small, grey automatic. It was a Webley .32 which had seen a lot of service. He loaded swiftly and with the casual precision of a chain-smoker lighting a cigarette. He put it into his hip pocket, which was so cut that it concealed the bulge. Seven bullets should be enough, whatever the emergency— but there wasn't likely to be an emergency where shooting would be necessary.

Was there?

They had used that car, which might have killed him.

Suzanne came, hurrying and bright as she opened the door. She saw the empty bed, and stopped on the threshold, arms raised in astonishment.

"*M'sieu!*"

"Close the door, *ma petite*," urged the Toff. As she did, he smiled broadly enough to dispense her sudden anxiety. "I'm going out. My injured leg is to fool some friends of mine—a practical joke, you see." He moved towards her, tilting her head, his forefinger placed on the point of her chin. She was such a child, with clear skin and beautiful eyes and great freshness. "Don't say a word to anyone, not even to Alphonse." Alphonse was the father of all porters in Nice. "Not to anyone," he insisted.

"I will not, *m'sieu*. But for you I am so glad!"

"Bless you," he said, in English; then added in French: "Go to the head of the stairs and the lift, and if the lift is on the move, or anyone is approaching, drop your keys with a bang. Understand?"

"Perfectly, *m'sieu!*"

"Wait two minutes, first."

"Yes," she said, and her eyes glowed because she liked sharing a practical joke with the English milord; all her life she would be sure that he was a milord. She went out, drab blue skirt swinging about nice legs.

Rollison opened another drawer, and took out a navy-blue beret, the colour faded to grey at the top, for it had seen a lot of wear. He pulled this on. It was not a disguise, but it made a startling difference. From the wardrobe he took an old, faded blue jacket, with a zip fastener up the front and elastic round the waist; and a pair of old, patched blue jeans. He drew all of these on, and inside the two minutes' grace that he had asked for he was at the door of his room.

He opened it an inch, and looked out. Suzanne dropped her keys with a metallic thump. He closed the door and stayed where he was. Then he heard the distant whine of the lift. It did not seem to stop at this floor. He opened the door again; there was Suzanne, standing at a point of vantage to see stairs, lift, and passages. She beckoned him with jerky, excited movements.

He went out, closing the door.

"But, *m'sieu*," Suzanne breathed, when she saw him again.

"Go back and tidy my room," Rollison said. "If anyone wants me, say that I'm having treatment for my leg, that I may have to go to hospital!" He gave her a wink which rivalled the prodigious one of Simon, then hurried along the passage. But he walked with curious gait, not like his own, and hunched his shoulders so that no one would have been surprised to hear that he was an electrician or a plumber or some artisan in the hotel on business which interested the customers only when it inconvenienced them.

A door leading off the end of the passage led to the service stairs and service lift. He chose the stairs. Luck so often favoured the bold. No one saw him until he was passing the open door of a huge kitchen, which looked like a palace built in stainless steel peopled by spacemen dressed in spotless white from the hem of their long aprons to the top of their stove-pipe hats. No one took any notice of the Toff. He went out of a service door, into a narrow cobbled street. A van stood outside, and men were unloading netting sacks of oranges, onions, green-leaved artichokes, and French beans. He moved swiftly towards the wider street at the end, and something glistened at his feet: the polish of his shoes.

He kicked into a pile of rubbish, smearing them, and hurried on.

He wanted a taxi, or better, but unlikely, a drive-yourself car; in it he would head as fast as he could for a headland which was very like the Cap Mirabeau, with one vital exception.

It was in the opposite direction from here.

Simon Leclair would be having a wasted journey. That was a little hard on Simon, but he was a married man with a married man's responsibilities, whereas the Toff was single.

The beggar had simply said that he thought he had seen the girl of the photograph in the grounds of the Villa Seblec, at a point called the Ile de Seblec.

The killer driver had given his address as the Villa Seblec.

.   .   .   .   .

The taxi moved away from the spot where it had dropped Rollison. The driver was not going far—just round the headland into some shade, drawn off the main road at a spot where he would not be noticed. He would doze there in the slothful warmth of midday, more than content with the five-thousand francs in his shabby leather wallet.

Rollison had known exactly where to come because of the beggar's directions. Now he studied the lie of the land in the shade of a glorious bush of bougainvillea, so deep and rich and flaming a red that it seemed to be born out of the sun. He stepped out into the burning heat, moving swiftly and sweating slightly. No one was in sight. This road was protected from the cliffs below by a low stone wall. The road wound out of sight, cut out of the side of the cliffs themselves.

A mile along, the beggar had told him, was a private road leading to the Ile de Seblec and two villas, one called Le Coc, the other the Villa Seblec. By climbing the wall by this mass of bougainvillea, and taking a precarious route over the

B

rocks, he would probably be able to reach the spit of land without being seen from the villas.

The beggar would be looking out for him.

Rollison climbed the wall. Below, the rugged cliff dropped almost sheer for two hundred feet; if he fell he would be thrown into the sea.

From here, it looked a deep, deep blue.

Rollison scrambled over pale grey rocks in which long, coarse grass grew, a few wild geraniums showed up vividly, and flowers he couldn't name grew from cracks in the rock. He would not be seen until he got near the sea, where Gaston the beggar would be waiting for him.

Gaston had told him that he had followed the raven-haired girl here, and watched—and seen Daphne Myall.

The heat was a worse enemy than the danger of being seen.

It came down from the sun; it rose from the rocks; and it seemed to rise out of that deep blue sea, which had a curious brassy look, although in the distance a faint haze obscured the sharpness of the horizon. Some way out, a single white yacht rode at anchor, graceful and still in the Mediterranean's midday sun.

Holding on to a rock here, finding a wobbly foothold there, Rollison moved with commendable speed. It did not seriously occur to him that he might fall. The bright green roof of one of the villas came in sight, and he paused. There was a dip in the rocky land ahead, enabling him to see; that probably meant that he could be seen if anyone were watching.

Why should they watch?

He scanned the rocky cliff, and saw no sign of movement or of man. A ginger cat was sitting in a little patch of shade, and had one eye open, watching him. He went on, more slowly and more cautiously, until the whole of the roof and part of the upper walls of the villa came in sight; suddenly he could see a window.

"Make for a spiky palm-tree, growing shoulder high," the

beggar had said. "I will place a cigarette packet there for you to see."

The stunted palm-tree was there, leaves thick and spiky, and looking as though the heat had drawn all the sap out of them. The cigarette packet? Rollison scanned the rocky hill-side, until he saw something white and blue, went towards it, and recognised it as a packet of Celtique. He didn't pick it up, but moved closer to the palm-tree. On the telephone the beggar had said that he had a hiding-place, just below the palm-tree, from which he could see the villa and the jetty, but could not be seen.

Rollison passed the palm-tree.

Beyond it the ground sloped sharply. He could see the jetty. He could see the villa. He could see the grounds, with small fountains playing, the lawns a beautiful, luscious green, rose-gardens, scarlet beds of geraniums and canna, hedges of flaming bougainvillea, of juniper and sweet honeysuckle, the scent of which was wafted on a gentle breeze. Paths wound their way about the garden, which was so beautiful that it was out of this world.

Between it and Rollison there was stark ugliness, touched with horror.

There was the battered body of the beggar.

.   .   .   .   .

The eyes, which had been such a beautiful velvety brown, were closed. A trickle of blood ran between them from the battered head. It was conceivable—just conceivable—that the man had fallen on his head and smashed his skull, but it was not likely. Rollison crouched there, very still, and watched; and clenched his teeth, for flies were swarming.

The beggar's body was broken, too; that showed from the twisted arms, and the odd angle at which he lay.

Rollison looked about him: first towards the silent house, set in that spurious beauty, then towards the road cut be-tween the rocks, then back along the path by which he had come. He saw no one. The cat was out of sight. There was just the hum of insects and, from below, the soft murmur of the sea. Yet he did not feel as if he were alone; he seemed to have more than death for company.

He went nearer to the beggar, crouching, knowing that no matter how low he crouched, until he was practically at the dead man's side he could be seen from the top windows of the villa. Had the beggar been seen by someone watching from there?

Was he being watched?

He reached the hollow where the beggar lay, and knelt beside him. He could neither see the villa nor be seen from it. He did not need to touch an outflung arm to check on death, and made a savage swing of his own arms, so that death should be left untormented. Teeth clenched tightly, he studied the head-wounds. He became quite sure that someone had come upon the beggar from behind, and battered him to death, then flung him down here. Almost certainly Gaston had been returning from the telephone call to Rollison.

Someone as certainly knew that Rollison was here.

That body, in all its pathetic loneliness, was a bait; and he was the fish that it was meant for. He had the same feeling as before, of being watched; he felt the creepiness that came with danger, running up and down his spine. He looked round again. No one was in sight, and yet——

He felt inside the dead man's pockets, drew out some papers, a pathetic wallet, and a creased and dirty photograph of a little child. That was everything, except for a few coins and the two thousand franc notes which Rollison had given him. Rollison put all these into his own pocket, then straightened up. He took off the blue jacket, stripped off his shirt and spread it over the battered head, fastening it down with small rocks. He put the jacket on again, and moved a little, so that he could see the villa.

He could see the jetty, too, and three dinghies, one small eighteen-foot yacht, its sails furled and riding at anchor, and a sleek cabin-cruiser. The white of the boats against the sea's cobalt blue made the scene like a photograph coloured by an expert. It couldn't be real.

Only the boats moved, gently; and two gulls, white as the paint on cabins and sides, swaying gently and lazily, as if they were having a doze in the heat.

Why was no one here?

The dead man had been followed to the telephone, the follower had guessed that he had sent for help—perhaps guessed whom he had called. Then the body had been left as bait.

Bait needed a fisherman at the end of a line; where was the fisherman? The silence, the fact that no one was in sight, added to the eeriness set in all this beauty.

Then Rollison heard a sound, from the house.

A scream.

5

THE GIRL WITH RAVEN-BLACK HAIR

THE scream came again, cutting across the silence like a slashing knife. Rollison crouched and watched, his thoughts wrenched from contemplation of death.

"*Eeeeeee!*" came the scream.

Rollison moved his right hand. The automatic appeared as if it had come out of the hip pocket of its own volition. He made himself turn full circle, making sure that no one was creeping up on him while he was distracted by the disturbance at the house.

No one was.

"*Eeeeeee!*" the cry came again, and he thought that it

sounded nearer. A door banged: only a door could make a sound like that. A man shouted. Footsteps sounded sharp and clear, those of a running woman and those of a running man—perhaps more than one man.

Rollison did not stand upright, but he wanted to.

Suddenly a girl appeared on the blue-tiled loggia at the side of the house. One moment all was still and empty, the next she appeared. She wore a wispy brassière and pale pink panties—and high-heeled shoes which were as red as the bougainvillea. Long, shapely legs moved swiftly; she was like a golden nymph—or she would have been but for the terror in her face. She ran towards the jetty, her black hair streaming behind her. Rollison, who was two hundred yards away, was quite sure that he knew her; she had wanted to speak to him on the promenade, but for some reason had not dared.

With what grace she ran!

Behind her thudded the beast.

A man, shorter and stockier than the girl, was obviously running with an effort; he limped badly and lumbered along. The girl outpaced him; she was drawing away noticeably with every stride. He was nearly bald, and his white coat was flying open and his tie streaming over his neck. What he lacked in inches and speed he made up in desperation. His footsteps sounded on the path behind the girl, like the thudding of a pile-driver on the bed of a river. His arms worked like pistons.

Another man appeared at the doorway, also running, but more slowly. He was older, frail-looking. He gave up running when he reached the path—just watched the others.

The girl was near the jetty. Every movement of her lithe young body was a moving picture. She was further away now, so that Rollison could not see her terror; although he could sense it—it was revealed in every movement that she made. The stocky man lumbered on, his arms still working. The girl reached the end of the jetty; in a few steps she would be at the edge, with only the sea in front of her.

She did not pause, but now raised her arms and held them straight out, as if about the dive. She did dive from the edge of the jetty, and towards two of the dinghies. Until then held and fascinated by the scene and by her rhythmic movement, Rollison was suddenly frightened for her. She was close to the dinghies; if she banged her head she would probably sink and not come up again.

She cleft the water, hardly making a splash; and the water was so clear that he could see the way she was shooting through it. She broke surface beyond the dinghies, and began to swim. Her strokes were like her running: smooth and rhythmic, not even hurried. It was as if she knew, even in her panic, that if she moved too quickly she would lose speed through the water. Her head moved from side to side. Whenever she lifted her face out of the water to breathe, she was facing Rollison. Her black hair was like paste now, sometimes flat over her forehead and eyes, sometimes brushed straight back by the water. She made no attempt to look behind her.

Rollison did.

The stocky man had stopped running, but was walking very quickly. It was like someone who had not full control of his legs, going downhill and afraid that he would pitch forward on his nose. Only his left arm was now jerking to and fro; his right was still.

He clattered on to the wooden jetty, and drew his right hand out of his pocket.

He had a gun.

"Oh, no," said the Toff, very softly.

The girl was some distance from the jetty, and swimming across a small bay towards another headland. There were other villas round that headland, and private beaches where she might wade ashore. But these were a long way off, and for minutes yet she would be within the stocky man's range. He was in no hurry, but levelled the gun, and obviously took careful aim.

The Toff shot at him.

At that distance, and with a small automatic, it wasn't easy to judge the right spot. He wanted to hit the gun-hand, and might get the shoulder or the chest. The bark of his shot sounded very loud. He saw the stocky man jerk round towards him; that was what he had feared. He saw the man flinch, stagger, and then sway towards the edge of the jetty. He'd been hit, but the Toff couldn't tell where. He had a nasty feeling that it was in a vital spot, for the man had no control over himself at all, was going to crumple up at any moment; and if he fell, he might fall into the sea.

The old man was staring towards Rollison, who still crouched out of sight.

The stocky man fell at last, on to the edge of the jetty. Something about the way he fell puzzled the Toff. He looked as if the natural way to fall would take him into the water, but his body twisted, and he fell safely; as if he'd planned it. He might not be as badly hurt as he had pretended. He was looking towards the spot where Rollison lay hidden, too.

The only sound was the splashing of the girl's arms. She was now a long way off, almost out of range of a pistol-shot. She was still swimming powerfully, and her hair looked like a shiny black bathing-cap.

More people arrived.

Rollison heard them at first, two men in a car which seemed to be moving too swiftly. He saw it swing into sight round a bend in the private road. Both men wore white or cream-coloured caps and were dressed in white. They sat together at the front of an open Cadillac all-weather, its cellulose glistening apple-green. They must have seen something of what had happened from the car, for as it jolted to a standstill at the back of the villa, both doors opened and the men jumped out. They went racing into the villa, and Rollison could hear their footsteps.

He didn't wait any longer.

He stood up, becoming visible from the grounds, and turned towards the sea. He could make his way towards it

and reach a spot near which the girl would have to pass on her
desperate swim to safety—but to do that he had to keep
within view of anyone at the jetty. He couldn't hurry on the
rocks, and didn't try. He kept glancing round at the man on
the jetty, who still lay in a heap. Then the others appeared,
with the old man. The sound of voices floated across to
Rollison, and the two newcomers ran towards the jetty.

The stocky man suddenly sprang up.

Rollison saw the movement, and guessed what was coming.
He flung himself down. Two shots came from the stocky
man's gun, bullets chipped the rocks close to Rollison's head.
He didn't move. The stocky man took fresh aim, and waited.
Rollison had felt a pluck at his coat; two or three inches
further in and the bullet would have taken his neck.

The two men were shouting.

The stocky man glanced towards them, and so made his big
mistake. Rollison fired. He didn't see where the bullet
struck, but the stocky man snatched his right arm away, as if
the gun in it had suddenly become red hot. The gun dropped,
struck the jetty, bounced a few inches, then slithered over
the side and dropped into the water. Rollison heard the plop
as it went in.

Rollison jumped to his feet, and began to move towards the
beach again. The girl was swimming rather less strongly,
apparently flagging. He watched closely, and sensed the
truth: she was fighting against a current, swimming straight
into it and finding it tough going. She must be touching the
depths of despair.

Rollison went down towards the beach, cursing the sharp
rocks and the difficulties of moving. He was slipping here,
or grabbing a plant or a rock to steady himself. When he
looked towards the jetty, he saw that the two newcomers were
climbing down into a little rowing-boat, tied to a stanchion.
The stocky man, holding his arm above the wrist, was watching them, and the frail old man had disappeared.

The newcomers would row to the cabin cruiser, and follow

the girl that way. She was swimming into that current, and wouldn't stand a chance of reaching land unless she could find a way out of it. If it exhausted her, it might draw her under; and even if she had the strength to keep fighting, she would be drawn remorsely back towards the launch.

Rollison clambered down.

The men, now in the rowing-boat, skimmed over the water towards the cruiser.

The girl seemed to be stationary, although her arms were moving and her head kept turning so that she faced the shore. She wasn't making an inch of progress, and was moving more slowly, as if genuinely afraid of what might happen if she stopped.

Rollison reached a spot high above a little sandy beach. To reach the beach he would have to jump fully thirty feet, and there were rocks below. He dared not risk it. He went further on, seeking another way down, almost at the point of the second headland. He could see villas on the east side, and another jetty some way off with boats riding at anchor.

A few yards further on was a possible way of getting down to another sandy beach. He quickened his pace, but still had to scramble. The Villa Seblec with its green roof fell out of sight. The only sound he could hear now was that of the movements he made—little stones falling, sandy soil trickling down.

The girl was too far off for the sound of her swimming to reach him. She——

He felt a sudden panic, for she was not in sight. It was as if someone he had known for a long, long time had been dragged under by that vicious current. His breath quickened, the clenching of his teeth hurt his jaw. He scrambled more quickly, reached a spot ten feet above the sand, and jumped.

As he landed, an engine spluttered.

He ran floundering across the sand, reached the jutting rocks and saw the girl, who had been hidden by them. She was now on her back, and her arms were moving over and over in the circular motion of a fine, expert back stroke. He guessed that she was using it because she was so tired.

It would never get her to safety.

The engine spluttered, fell silent, then spluttered again; suddenly it developed the steady roaring note which meant that it was turning over smoothly. The men in it would soon be on the move. It had taken the girl fifteen minutes or more to get to the spot where she was now; the men in the launch might take five. *Five*. The girl was a hundred yards offshore, and the current sweeping round the headland kept her away from it; without help, she simply wouldn't be able to get away.

There was no time for Rollison to swim to help her.

He took off the jacket and the jeans, kicked off his shoes, tucked the automatic into the toe of one, then waded into the warm sea, knee deep in a few strides. He plunged forward. The men in the launch, looking straight ahead, hadn't seen him; nor had the girl, who was still swimming on her back. The launch engine was beating levelly; soon it would be close to her, and she would have no hope.

6

FOUR AT SEA

ROLLISON swam powerfully. There was no current here; or if there were, it helped him. When he raised his head, he could see the launch, almost straight ahead; and all the time the chugging of the engine travelled clearly over the water.

He could not see the girl, but saw that the launch was

slowing down: the note of the engine changed, and it was turning a wide circle, to search for the girl. The Toff dived. For a few seconds the bows pointed almost directly at him, as if he had been seen and the men were heading for him. When he surfaced, he could see one of them leaning against the side of the launch, back towards him.

They were looking towards the girl.

Was she still swimming?

Rollison dropped into a fast crawl, and seemed to skim the water rather than go through it. The cruiser loomed up, much closer, with the little dinghy bobbing along behind. When the Toff stopped that furious burst of speed he was only a few yards away from it.

The engine of the cruiser had been cut out.

Ropes dangled from the stern, because the two men had been in too much of a hurry to pull them aboard. One dragged softly through the water, and there was the usual soft lapping sound.

Rollison heard a loud splash, as if one of the men had dived overboard; it was impossible to be sure. He trod water until he was able to breathe more steadily, then gripped the dangling rope and began to haul himself up. It wasn't far and it wasn't difficult. When his head was level with the deck, he raised one hand and gripped the railing which protected the stern. Then he hoisted himself up, and peered on to the cruiser.

No one was inside.

The cabin and the engine-house superstructure were between him and the two men. The boat was drifting, but there was not even the suspicion of a roll. Rollison climbed up and over, water streaming off him. He stared at the pool he made, and at the puddle that formed after a single footstep. He would leave a trail which might be seen at a single glance. He glanced round, saw nothing that would help to mop up or to dry himself. He pulled off his singlet, wrung it out, and began to rub himself down.

Men were talking quietly, in French. So both were aboard.

Rollison wrung the singlet out again, and then mopped up the water on the deck; the sun would dry the little that was left. He tossed the singlet out to sea, then cursed himself, for the splash sounded very loud. He stared towards the super-structure, which was made of beautifully polished wood, but no one appeared.

He heard one man say: "Together, now, pull hard."

Was the girl at the end of a rope? Or a life-belt? Rollison couldn't guess, and it no longer worried him; they hadn't been alarmed by the splash he'd made. He walked across the deck, and the heat of the scrubbed boards stung his feet. He reached the engine-room; over the polished wood, which was hot enough to make him wince. He crept towards the end of the engine-house, and found himself at a little gang-way between the engine and the cabin. The cabin was approached by a flight of wide stairs, and he glimpsed luxury below.

He reached the edge of the gangway.

Both men were hauling at a rope, and putting a lot of effort into it. There wasn't much doubt that the girl was at the other end. One man's hair was black, and brushed down tightly; and there was a look of the driver of the killer Renault about him.

They paused.

One of them spoke, but what he said didn't reach the Toff. The other leaned on the rope. Then the man who had spoken bent over the rail and began to pull.

The girl's head appeared; in spite of the water, it still glistened like jet. Her shoulders gleamed a beautiful golden brown. It was impossible to tell whether she was conscious or not.

Rollison could move now, and the men wouldn't have a chance. He could pick up the spanner from the engine-casing and crack their skulls, as the beggar's had been cracked. He could knock them out, and could pitch them overboard. In that moment he felt that he hated them both, that nothing would be more than they deserved.

He watched.

The man leaning over was grunting. He had his arms beneath the girl's, but she was too heavy for him to lift over the rail. The other man dropped the rope and went to help; but it took experience and skill to lift a dead weight over the deck's rail, and they had neither.

The Toff turned, went down the stairs—stairs, not gangway, was the word. They were carpeted in deep red, and the carpet had thick pile. At the foot was a door leading into a saloon, or lounge, and a passage seemed to run right round this saloon, with more doors leading off it.

The Toff heard the sounds of the men above his head as he took a quick look round.

The saloon was surprisingly spacious. The door was open, and showed the corner of a tiny chromium bar, with a mirror behind it, upholstered seats round the walls and several low chairs and tables. The whole place had an air of opulence.

Rollison glanced inside, and saw photographs on the walls —all beautiful studies of girls, mostly in the nude.

He moved out of the main saloon, and stepped along the passage. This ran right round the main cabin, and formed a square with one side missing. A narrow door led off each side, and when he opened one, he saw two bunks, one atop the other. The others were the same, so the cruiser could sleep six with comfort. He didn't know where the crews' quarters or the galley was, and didn't trouble to find out, for he heard a thud on deck.

Then came footsteps; they were bringing the girl down.

The footsteps were slow and heavy; sliding noises came with them from time to time. Were the men so badly out of condition? Rollison stood in the passage behind the saloon, out of sight of the stairs. He heard the couple when they reached the head of the stairs and when they started down.

One man was gasping for breath. There were more thumping and bumping sounds before they stopped moving, and Rollison judged that they were at the door of the saloon.

A man said gaspingly: "Where shall we take her?"

"To the bunks—shall we?"

They paused, still gasping, until one of them said· "No, in here, I think. We shall take her ashore when we get back, it will not be so long."

More sound of movement came, and seemed much closer. Rollison didn't move. He heard them go inside the saloon. When silence fell, he guessed that they had laid the girl on the floor. After a moment there was the unmistakable sound of clinking glasses; one of them was pouring out drinks.

There were the usual platitudinous comments. Gradually the heaving breathing quietened. A man chuckled.

"She nearly got away."

"She has courage," the other said.

"Courage—pst!" There was a pause. "After this, she will not try to cheat us again."

The other man didn't speak, and Rollison sensed constraint between them. That was a pity. The more they talked, the more he was likely to learn, and he had come down here and let them bring her so that he could have a chance to listen-in.

Matches scraped.

"Sautot has a very bad hand," said the man who had remarked upon the girl's courage. "The bullet went right through it. Ugh! The blood made me sick. He will not be any use for a little while."

"Don't you believe it; Sautot is tough." This was the man who had sneered at the girl's courage; he had dark hair, unless the Toff had missed his guess. "He'll soon be all right. Old Morency was very frightened, too. He is no use, that one; too old."

"He has been very good."

"Gérard," said the sneering man, "when are you going to

learn that there is no room for sentiment? He is old, he will soon be useless, and one day he will be snuffed out."

There was a full minute of silence before the same man went on:

"It is a good thing we got the girl; if we had lost her, Chicot would have been like a fiend."

The voices were muffled by the wall of the saloon and by the distance; and yet in the way the man said 'Chicot would have been like a fiend' there was a different note from anything that had gone before. Fear? Awe? It was something like that. Chicot mattered; Chicot could afford to rage, and the possibility that he would worried even the man who sneered at the girl's courage.

Violette.

The Toff remembered her when she had come for the audition. She was not as beautiful as some, but most beautifully made, with a skin as lovely as the skin of a fresh peach. She had deep, violet eyes, so was well-named. Now she lay on the floor of the saloon, and the Toff did not know whether she was hurt, or unconscious, or conscious and terrified.

He did not even know if she was dead.

One man said: "It is time we start back, Gérard. Will you go and start the engine?"

The other man didn't answer. That sense of estrangement was noticeable again, quite unmistakable. The sneering man was Raoul, the other Gérard; and clearly Gérard didn't trust Raoul.

"You will not hurt her," he said at last.

"Why should I, you fool?" Raoul said tartly. "Look at her; she is half dead. Go and start the engine; I'll get some blankets for her."

The man named Gérard still didn't move.

"What is the matter with you?" Raoul sounded ill-tempered.

"My friend," said Gérard quietly, "you remember what Sautot said. He was questioning her about this letter to the

Englishman, Rollison, who calls himself the agent of Rambeau. And he was—hurting her."

"Why be squeamish?" Raoul rasped. Rollison could remember the way he had looked when at the wheel of the Citroen. "He was making her talk, wasn't he? If he had to twist her arm or bend her finger back to make her open her mouth, what does it matter? What is your trouble, Gérard?" The constraint was near the open now; they weren't far from a sharp quarrel. "Does she mean anything to you? Do you wish to have her for yourself? Is that it?"

Gérard didn't answer.

"Because if it is," sneered Raoul, "Chicot will be *very* interested."

"Raoul," said Gérard softly, "don't you do anything to her. Understand? Sautot had his orders, to find out how much she had said to this Rollison, but you haven't any. You don't know what he was trying to find out from her. Wait until we get back, and telephone Chicot for orders. Make sure of that, because you might do the wrong thing."

Silence fell.

"I won't hurt her," Raoul said.

After a moment's pause, more movement followed. Gérard left the saloon and walked briskly up the stairs. Odd noises began soon after he reached the engine.

There was no sound inside the saloon, and Rollison made none.

He had learned a little, and it might become a great deal. Chicot was the man they feared. Sautot was the stocky man with a bullet-hole through his right hand. Morency—a name which might be English or American—was the old man, and a doctor. These two were Raoul and Gérard, and they knew that Sautot had been questioning the girl when she had escaped and run, screaming, to a desperate hope of safety.

Violette——

Rollison found himself smiling at thought of her grace.

Then the engine started.

It ran more smoothly from the first note this time, and in a few seconds they would be on their way. It wasn't far back to the jetty.

He moved round to the saloon, trying to remember whether it was possible to glance down the stairs and see the front door of the saloon. He didn't think so. He was nearly sure that Gérard would look down, trying to make certain that Raoul was not 'questioning' the girl. There wasn't much that Raoul would stop at.

Rollison reached the doorway, and peered inside.

Raoul stood with his feet apart, his right elbow crooked, as if he had a glass in his hand. His sleek black hair was slightly out of place—not very much, just ruffled out of its usual sleekness. He wore a biscuit-coloured suit, like the driver of the Citroen; beyond doubt it was the same man.

The girl lay on the floor, with two blue rugs over her. Her feet showed at one end, and she had lost her shoes. Her hair was lank and wet, and a large dark patch on the carpet seemed to be spreading. She faced the door, and her head lolled. She looked as if she were unconscious; but Rollison saw that her eyes were flickering.

Suddenly Raoul moved.

He flung the contents of his glass into the girl's face. She gasped, her body heaved, her eyes opened wide, and her hands appeared, and she put them to her face. Raoul bent down on one knee, snatched at her right wrist, and twisted savagely. The blankets fell back from her lovely shoulders. She was held in a torturing grip—the kind of grip she had tried to escape when in the villa.

"Now you'll tell me what was in that letter to Rollison," Raoul said in a voice which only just reached the Toff. "Tell me, or I'll break your arm."

He sounded as if he meant it.

If the Toff went in now, a shout would bring Gérard running.

7

VIOLETTE

THE greatest danger would come from the girl.

She lay there helpless, mouth open in a strangely muted scream. Her head was raised. Raoul knelt between her and the Toff, who could see her so plainly that he knew that if she caught a glimpse of movement she would give him away.

"What was in the letter?" growled Raoul, and a slight movement of his wrist made her gasp; he clapped his right hand over her mouth, to silence the sound, twisted again, and then took his hand away. "*What was in it?*"

"I asked him to see me," she gasped; "that is all, everything."

Raoul didn't believe her.

Rollison was inside the room now, behind the man. If Violette looked up she would see him. There were only seconds to spare, for Gérard might come at any moment. The Toff moved, swift as a gust of wind, and his hands were stretched out to grasp Raoul by the neck.

Violette saw it.

She gasped again and her gaze shifted; Raoul couldn't fail to understand that someone was there. He would expect Gérard. He sprang to his feet, twisting round as he did so; and the Toff stopped clutching at his neck, just clenched a fist and smashed it into his chin.

Raoul toppled backwards. He caught a leg against Violette, and fell. He banged his head on the edge of the shiny bar, a bottle quivered and rattled against two glasses. One toppled. Raoul slithered down the wall, and Rollison went after him, reached him, struck again.

Once . . .

Twice.

Raoul slumped down inert, the little gasp coming as he fell. He didn't move, but lay between Violette and the wall, eyes closed and mouth slightly open, but very slack. There was a trickle of blood at his lips and chin.

The girl just raised her hand towards the Toff, as if wanting to hug him in the ecstasy of her relief. Long, bare, shapely arms——

Rollison took her hands and squeezed.

"Lie still," he warned; "don't make a sound."

He moved towards the bar, and picked up one of the bottles. It was whisky; either Raoul or Gérard didn't share Simon Leclair's tastes. Holding it like a club, Rollison went to the door. The thing he dreaded was to see Gérard peering down, but there was no sign of him. The engine was chugging away peacefully; the cruiser seemed to be going at a good clip.

Rollison started up the stairs.

He could see Gérard's back, bent over the engine, as if there were something amiss, after all. He reached the deck.

Gérard was fiddling with something, with that peculiar application of born engineers. His head was on one side, as if he were listening for a faint irregularity in the beat of the engine. Rollison looked only at him, but not far away there was the green-topped villa and the beautiful garden, the jetty and the other craft.

Other men, too?

Rollison couldn't see over the roof of the engine-house without making himself visible to anyone watching from the house or the jetty. He didn't stand upright, but took another step towards the man at the engine.

Gérard straightened up.

"Gérard," said Rollison very softly.

The youth started violently, and turned his head. He was fair-haired, fresh-faced, open-mouthed; no ghost could have affected him more than the sight of Rollison then. He didn't move, but leaned further back. The engine purred, and the green-topped villa seemed to draw nearer.

"Who—who—who—" began Gérard, and gulped in desperation. "Who——"

"Gérard," said the Toff, still softly, "turn her round. We're not going back to the Ile de Seblec, we're going to Cap Mirabeau. Head her out to sea, get the right bearing, and then lash the helm."

"Bu—bu—bu——" began Gérard.

"Or I'll smash your head in," Rollison said, and raised the whisky bottle.

The youth turned, too frightened even to shout or to argue. He touched the helm. There was nothing to stop him from heading straight for the jetty, ramming it, making sure that they couldn't get away. He didn't. He glanced over his shoulder once, at the near-naked figure of the Toff, who was holding the bottle as if it were a club. The cabin-cruiser swung round in a sweeping arc, and then headed south from the big bay. Out at sea there was little danger; in the bay there were so many small boats that he dare not leave the cruiser with her helm lashed. Later, to reach Cap Mirabeau, they would have to swing inshore and head for a spot where there was plenty of anchorage and public as well as private jetties. Now the Toff needed time more than anything else. He looked round, tensely.

No one was in the grounds of the villa, which lay burning in the sun. The heat rose in a shimmering haze from the tiled roof, from the paths, from the water itself. Never had water looked so blue as it did close to the *Maria*. The *Maria*, the Toff repeated to himself, and saw the name painted in gilt letters on a lifebelt fastened to the top of the engine-house.

He felt the fair-haired youth's pocket for a gun, and found only an ordinary pen-knife. He took this, then watched the distant, open sea.

Gérard turned his head, and Rollison had a feeling that he

had seen him before. He was scared out of his wits, yet there was something almost attractive about him. Seen sunning himself on the pebbles at Nice, or sun-bathing aboard one of the yachts at Cannes, one would have noticed him and thought 'nice lad'. His hair was very fair and very curly; he had the kind of skin that never really tanned, yet didn't redden.

"Are you—are you *Rollison*?"

"Am I?" murmured the Toff, and added very softly: "Look where you're going."

Gérard turned his head back.

"Lash the helm."

"I—I am about to," said Gérard. 'Lash' was too strong a word; there was a loop of rope nearby, and a row of wooden pins; he put the loop over one of the pins, so that the wheel couldn't move, and then turned round again. "What are you going to do when we——"

The Toff struck him beneath the jaw.

.   .   .   .   .

"Hallo, Violette," said the Toff, reaching the saloon and smiling amiably at the girl. "Feeling better?" She was sitting on the edge of the wall seat, and had been watching Raoul, who hadn't moved. "You won't know yourself when we get ashore. There's another one—Gérard by name. Know him?"

It was good to feel that he could relax, even for a few minutes.

The girl said huskily: "Raoul is the bad one."

"I don't think we ought to be too sorry for Gérard yet," said Rollison dryly.

He started to drag the unconscious Gérard into the saloon, but changed his mind. Raoul was stirring, but would be too dazed to be dangerous for a while.

"I'll be back," Rollison said. He edged his way out of the saloon, still holding Gérard by the shoulders, then dragged him to the nearest of the three bunk-rooms. The porthole

was too small for men of the size of Gérard and Raoul to
squeeze through. He lugged Gérard inside, and hoisted him
to the upper bunk.

He went back for Raoul.

Violette was standing near the dark-haired man, with a
bottle in her hand. Hatred showed in her eyes. She had a
rug draped round her shoulders, she shivered, and yet she
looked strangely magnificent; as a Red Indian squaw might
look with a tribal blanket round her shoulders and eyes
ablaze with the fire of war.

"He tried to get up," she said thinly.

"Try to find some string," Rollison said briskly. "Strong
stuff, please; cord would be better. Once they're tied up we
can take it easier."

"I know where to find some," Violette said. "I will go
and get it."

She stepped towards the door. The rug cloak could not
hide the animal grace with which she walked. She seemed
strong again, and able to do whatever she wished. She went
up the stairs towards the engine-house, legs smooth and
rounded, ankles beautifully defined. Rollison watched her—
and Raoul tried to scramble to his feet.

"Don't be silly," said the Toff, and pushed him heavily
against the wall. Raoul flopped. "If you really want to get
hurt, try tricks like that. Who is Chicot?"

Raoul opened his mouth, and closed it again. There had
been fear in the girl's eyes, but no greater than that in
Raoul's.

"I said, who is Chicot?" Rollison repeated.

"I—I don't know," muttered Raoul, and tried to look
anywhere but into Rollison's eyes. "I don't know!"

"You know what trick you tried to start with Violette, don't
you?" murmured Rollison. "I could try it on you. In fact
I'd like to try it on you now. I'd like you to know what it
feels like to know your arm is being broken. What it feels like
when a car is leaping at you, and you don't think you've a

second more to live." His eyes were very hard, and no man could look more deadly. "Who is Chicot?" he asked softly.

Raoul tried to push the question away, actually made a motion with his hand. He opened his mouth, but words wouldn't come.

"Chicot is—the—the great one."

"The great what?"

"He—he is the leader," Raoul said, but he hesitated over the word leader, and then burst out into English: "You understand, he is the boss!"

"I understand," said Rollison, now quite mildly. "Does he live at the Villa Seblec?"

"No! He—he comes there sometimes; he—he has many names." Raoul was sweating, and it was not all due to the heat of the cabin. "Chicot is what we call him, but only Chicot. Who he is I do not know."

That could be true.

"What does he look like?" demanded the Toff.

"He is—he is just a man, smaller—smaller than you. *Ordinary!*" The word burst out.

The Toff looked into the frightened eyes for fully thirty seconds, then decided that if Raoul were to talk more freely, it would have to be later. He took the man's arm, turned him round, and thrust him towards the door.

Violette was coming down.

She had left the rug on deck, and wore only the flimsies. Her hair hung lank yet gleaming down her back, beginning to show signs of curling under the drying warmth. She carried a coil of cord over her arm, and a knife in her hand. It wasn't her beauty of figure or the way she moved that impressed the Toff; it was the way she looked at Raoul, as if she would gladly thrust that knife into him. The desire was so obvious, the hatred so naked, that Raoul actually cringed away.

"Go on," Rollison said; "she won't hurt you—yet."

He pushed the youth towards the cabin, where Gérard already lay. Gérard was coming round, but was still dazed.

He remained like that while Rollison tied his ankles together, and then his wrists. He left him on the upper bunk, and turned to Raoul. He tied Raoul's wrists more tightly than he had Gérard's; he felt, like Violette, the brutal desire to hurt. He left the men trussed up, and went out with Violette, feeling vaguely dissatisfied, although so much had been done to give him cause for satisfaction.

He said: "Now we can have a drink, and relax. I'll make sure where we're going first, and then——"

She raised her hands, and her eyelids flickered.

"We have——" she muttered thickly. Then her eyes closed and she fell forward into the Toff's arms. Her body was heavy, her arms bent in front of her in a strange, huddled posture. For a moment Rollison just stood supporting her; then he smiled gently, shifted her, lifted her, and carried her into the saloon. It was collapse from the strain, and would do her no harm. He covered her with the rug, then picked up the knife she had dropped and went up on deck.

They were well out in the bay, and Nice was still in sight, white buildings clear against the grey shape of the coast. He altered the helm, so that they didn't head too far out to sea, but ran parallel with the coast itself. He didn't feel so good, and two things were the matter with him—the first, hunger. It was after two o'clock, and his only breakfast had been coffee and rolls; in Nice one did as the Frenchmen do. The other thing, that sense of dissatisfaction was less tangible; surely it couldn't be with anything that he had done.

It had been the kind of success that made one wonder when the luck was going to turn and the outlook darken. But the immediate outlook was as clear as the blue Mediterranean sky.

He went back into the saloon, took a cigarette from a packet which had been left on the bar, lit it, and contemplated Violette. He found ice in a small ice-box behind the bar, rang a cloth out in chilled water, bathed her face and forehead. Then he put a spoonful of brandy to her lips.

She swallowed, and her eyes flickered.

He watched her closely. There was some quality about this girl, which wasn't only to do with her looks or her figure. She had a kind of natural shamelessness, as if she was proud of her body and did not mind who knew it or who saw it.

She opened her eyes. He gave her a spot more brandy, told her to lie still, and went into the cabin where the prisoners were. He looked at Raoul, and knew how terrified Raoul was; but he didn't speak as he began to untie the knots at his wrists. Raoul's teeth chattered; he just couldn't stop himself. Rollison simply loosened the knots, and left them secure and went out without a word.

One could hate a sadist without imitating his methods.

Rollison went on deck again. No other craft was in sight. He felt happier.

He poked around, and found the tiny galley, with a built-in refrigerator and a built-in larder, behind the engine-house; and near it were two bunks, for the crew. He opened the larder door, and his eyes brightened; here was food. There was even bread, some croissants which felt fresh, like this morning's bake, some butter was in the 'fridge—and a tin of ham—everything he needed. He opened the tin, sliced ham, laid a tray, and carried it jauntily down to the saloon, placed it on a table, and looked upon Violette. She seemed almost herself again.

"We'll eat first and drink after," he said. "But I'd better go up and switch the engine off before we start. We'll drop anchor." He buttered a croissant, bit a piece off, winked at her, and went hurrying up the stairs.

He started for the stern and the anchor, heard another engine, looked towards the distant shore, and saw a launch bearing down upon the *Maria*.

Standing in the thwarts were two *gendarmes*.

8

VIOLETTE EXPLAINS A LETTER

ONE *gendarme* was fat, the other thin. They were approaching very fast, and into the slight wind, which had carried away the sound of their approach. Rollison stood and watched, his teeth clamped together. There was no doubt that they were bearing down on the *Maria*. At four hundred yards the fat one put a pair of binoculars to his eyes.

Rollison moved slowly to the engine-house, and deliberately switched off. Few things had ever cost him more effort; now nothing could stop the men from coming aboard. If he had made a run for it, he might have got ashore before they could catch up with him.

He'd taken his chance.

The *Maria* began to slow down. The launch with the two *gendarmes* was now only two hundred yards away. The tall policeman turned to the lean one, and said something; the other nodded.

Was this the vessel they were after?

The only reassuring thing was the fact that their revolvers stayed in their holsters.

The fat man bent down and picked up a megaphone. Rollison's French was good enough to understand nautical terms in spite of the distortion of the great horn.

"How many people have you on board?"

"Two, *messieurs!*" called Rollison, cupping his hands to make the words carry. His heart thumped, but his voice was steady. "*Mademoiselle, et moi aussi!*"

"Where is *mademoiselle?*"

Rollison hesitated.

He couldn't even begin to guess what this was about; the questions gave him hope that the police would not come

aboard—unless they found new reasons for suspicion.
Violette in a *bikini* would not cause a moment's surprise;
nylon flimsies might be a different matter.

"Below deck!" he called.

"We wish to see her."

"I'll tell her to come." Rollison turned away.

His heart was beating with steady, threatening thuds. The
police might be looking for Violette. They might be intend-
ing to come aboard, just fooling him by pretending that
they weren't in any great hurry.

He called down the saloon.

"Violette, will you come on deck?"

"A moment," she answered, so quickly that he guessed
that she had heard the shouting. At least she wouldn't be
taken by surprise. The steadiness of her voice was a help,
too. If she draped a rug round her—but would that make
sense? The sun was so hot that flimsies would look more
reasonable than a woollen rug.

He turned back to the launch.

It was coming up from the stern, after encircling the
Maria, and was much nearer. The police could come alongside and on board at any moment. At closer quarters the fat
man looked tough and leathery, and the lean one wiry. Both
had shiny brown belts and holsters, with the revolvers easy
to get at. A man at the helm of the launch was just another
sailor, wearing a faded blue blouse and a pair of jeans. His
blue beret was pushed to the back of his head. He could turn
that launch almost in its own length.

Rollison heard the girl coming.

He didn't look round, but scanned the faces of the policemen for signs of surprise; and saw none. There was the same
emotion on each; the look on their faces was the look of any
man seeing Violette for the first time. The Toff turned to
look at her.

She was very, very good; and his heart warmed.

She wore a fantastic modern beach-suit in the new fashion

which looked like a harlequin's dress. It was of jade-green colour, with splashes of gold, covering all of her lovely body. She might as well have appeared without a stitch on, she caused the same kind of sensation.

She looked at the two *gendarmes*; and in her eyes was a kind of promise.

Was she aware of that? Did she know that she seemed to promise so much?

"Hallo, Violette," said Rollison with commendable calm, and turned back to smile at the *gendarmes*. They had recovered from the sensation, but the moment when the man in each had pushed the policeman aside would live forever. "They want to speak to you."

The fat policeman said: "That is not the lady we are looking for. Have you seen a boat, like yours, named the *Nuit Verte*?"

"*Nuit Verte*," echoed Rollison, and found himself translating. "Green Night? No. But then, I haven't seen a cabin cruiser at all. I've had the helm lashed and have been below most of the time. Who's aboard her?"

"A young lady," said the fat policeman, all his suspicion apparently gone. "One Mademoiselle Bourcy. So ——" H_ held a hand at shoulder height. "No so tall as madame, not so——" He made a delightful gesture with his big clumsy hands and somehow managed to make it seem quite natural. "With fair hair—hair the colour of corn when it is cut."

Gérard had hair that colour.

So had the girl sitting next to Raoul in the Citroen that morning.

"No," said Rollison, "I haven't seen anyone like that. Have you, Violette?"

Violette looked down at the policemen as if at the most handsome men in the world.

"No, Richard," she murmured.

"If you pass the *Nuit Verte*, inform the nearest *commissariat de police* at once, if you please," said the fat man. He touched his peaked helmet. *"M'sieu–Madame!"* The lean policeman echoed the last two words, and the man at the helm formed them vaguely with his lips. Then the launch sheered off, and Rollison turned to look into Violette's eyes. He knew that they were quite as beautiful as he had told himself before.

"Where do you keep the other Dior models?" he asked.

Her smile was just a flash of fine white teeth and of red lips. This was the first time that he had seen her without some kind of fear. The transformation seemed to have come with her clothes; she was gay, she was *happy*. Well, who could blame her? She had been through an ordeal by fear, she'd been rescued, she had fainted. When she had come round, she had heard the men talking, and somehow steeled herself to make another effort, and she had made it. Now, relief from tension, from urgent fear, showed in a gaiety that would probably fade as quickly as it had come.

"There are several," she said; "apparently they always keep some clothes on board." She eyed Rollison much as a man might eye a girl whom he had not really seen before. Her eyes had a kind of radiant mockery, as if she knew that she was doing to him what he should be doing to her. She made him conscious of his lean, muscular body, of the tan of his skin; and he smiled almost warily into her face. Her eyes laughed. "There is plenty even for you, *m'sieu*."

"Naked and unashamed," said the Toff, "I am going to eat first; I'm hungrier than it's good to be. Would you care to stay up here and look for the *Nuit Verte?*"

"Later," said Violette, and moved and touched his arm. The radiance and the gaiety had vanished, shadows came back to her eyes. What had brought them back so suddenly? "M'sieu Rollison," she said, "I owe you so much; I owe you everything. I can never thank you."

But she tried.

She took his arms and pulled him close, and kissed him

fiercely, almost savagely. She willed him to put his arms around her, to add to the pressure of her sudden passion.

Then they moved apart.

Without a word, Rollison led the way to the saloon, to the . succulent ham and the fresh croissants, the unsalted butter and a Camembert cheese which was almost a dream.

As it was almost a dream, anchored here, a few miles off Nice, between the place where he had seen death, and the place where he had sent Simon Leclair. He hadn't thought of Simon for a long time. He wondered if the clown would ever know the whole truth of what had happened. He didn't say much, and the mood of quietness was upon them both. There were a hundred things he wanted to know, but he had plenty of time to ask his questions; and he wanted Violette to begin to talk of her own free will.

She did.

"Last night," she said, "I heard them plotting to kill you. There was Raoul, Morency and one other man, named Sautot. Morency is the English one." She spoke as if Rollison knew all of these people, she had but to name them; and she looked into his eyes.

"What had I done to offend them?" Rollison asked mildly.

"You search for the girl, Daphne Myall," Violette said flatly.

"Is she at the Villa Seblec?"

Violette shook her head, very slowly.

"No," she said. "At least, I have not seen her there, and I live there. Why do you want her?"

Rollison said: "Her parents are nice people."

The girl closed her eyes, as if that hurt. Rollison waited, convinced that it would be better if she volunteered everything she had to say.

She opened her eyes.

"That is a very good reason," she said. "You will not believe it, but it is because of very nice parents that I am here, and in such danger."

Rollison didn't speak.

"My own parents," Violette went on. "They did not deserve to suffer, *m'sieu*, but suffer they did. Their other daughter, Marie, disappeared like this Daphne Myall. Then it was discovered that her good name and that of our parents had been used to swindle a man of a large fortune." Violette paused, and shrugged. "She was last seen in Nice, at the *Baccarat* Club. Then she vanished. I came to look for her."

Rollison said quietly: "And you haven't found her yet?"

"No," said Violette. "I have not."

"What have you found?"

Violette said bitterly: "I thought I had found happiness. I was fascinated, enraptured, blinded. I fell in love with— the Devil."

The way she spoke told Rollison that this was as she felt. He murmured: "This Chicot?"

The name seemed to hurt.

"What do you know of him?"

"The two men are frightened of him."

"Yes, everyone becomes frightened of Chicot," Violette told him slowly. "It was Chicot who made such a fool of me. I met him at the Villa Seblec, inquiring for Marie. When I think of it, I feel that he exerted a kind of spell. It was not his looks—they are not remarkable—but a kind of magic——"

She meant it.

Rollison waited.

She said abruptly: "I stayed there, with him. That was for some weeks. I allowed myself to be dominated by him. I lent myself to a plot in which an old man was swindled of a great sum of money. Old men are so credulous when a woman is beautiful," she added wearily.

"All men," Rollison murmured.

She said: "Then I began to realise what I had done, but I was trapped, *m'sieu*. I could not leave Chicot or the Villa without my share in the great swindle being revealed. That would hurt my parents so much more, and I stayed, telling them that I still searched for Marie."

She turned away.

He did not force his questions, then.

.　　.　　.　　.　　.

The fans were on in the saloon. There was a kind of air-conditioning, which helped to cool the air. They had finished a meal, and had long drinks in front of them; hers a squash, his a lager. She still wore the harlequin beach-suit that was all concealing, and he had drawn on a pair of white shorts which he had found in the galley. It was cool, and they were well fed. But not for a moment had they been free from tension.

"Violette," he said quietly, "I've some questions—and some may hurt."

"I will answer if I can," she promised.

"This Chicot—is he at the Villa now?"

"No."

"Doesn't he live there?"

"No—he visits us sometimes."

"What is he like?"

She hesitated. "To look at first, just an ordinary little man," she said. "Nice, perhaps, with curly hair. Almost a boy, so innocent. What is your word?"

"Cherubic?"

"Exactly!" She was almost eager. "Then afterwards—so very cruel."

"Did he trap your sister, too?"

"I think so."

"Have you seen her at the Villa?"

"No."

"Other girls?"

She shrugged.

"They come—and they go."

"Where do they go?"

C

"That is what I cannot answer," Violette told him. "There is something I do not understand. They come, they are gay and happy—and then they disappear. I have tried to find out where, but I cannot."

"Are you still on good terms with Chicot?"

She flushed.

"I was, until recently."

"What happened then?"

She said: "I was told to visit you, to find out what you wanted. I tried to. When I was back at the Villa, Chicot was there. I have never seen him or any man so angry." She raised her hands, almost in self-defence. "How he raged—against *you*."

Rollison said sharply: "But why?"

"Some danger that you brought."

"But I'd never heard of Chicot!"

"You were here, you were looking for a missing girl. You brought danger. You had to be killed; Raoul and Gérard or Sautot must do that, so—I wanted to warn you."

"Why didn't you?"

Very simply she said, "Because I was afraid."

.   .   .   .   .

On deck there was just the heat, the silence, the distant shore, and all about them the deep blue sea.

Rollison made sure that no other boat was near, and went below again.

.   .   .   .   .

"I was afraid, and so was Madeleine," said Violette. "You saw her, perhaps?"

"I saw a fair-haired woman near you on the promenade, trying to attract my attention."

"I do not mean her," said Violette; "unless it was one who was anxious to see M. Rambeau's agent. Madeleine sat in the car, beside Raoul."

Rollison could recall that fair girl and her terror.

"Yes, I remember," he said.

"She is Raoul's wife," said Violette, "and also Gérard's sister. In the car she knew that Raoul tried to kill you. She ran away, but they caught her. I do not know what will happen to her now."

"What do you think will happen?" Rollison asked sharply.

"I think she will be killed, or she will be sent to Algiers," Violette answered. "I am not sure, but I have noticed much and heard a little. I believe that some of these girls drown themselves because of some shame; and others are sent——" She stood up quickly. "Come with me, please." She led the way to the deck.

They were just within sight of Nice and of the headlands. Violette did not look towards the land. She turned towards the south, put a hand upon his arm, and went on as if she were continuing a sentence started only a moment ago: "Perhaps you will find this Daphne Myall, poor Madeleine, and my sister Marie far across there, m'sieu. In Algiers there are many white girls, all trying to forget. I—*I* would rather die. I think I shall have to die," she added.

Something in the way she looked stifled the protest on Rollison's lips.

9

GÉRARD

ROLLISON looked at her, without smiling, until his lips curved and a gleam appeared in his eyes. He could take this solemnly, as she was doing, or could try to kill the thought of death stone dead.

"If I were you," he said, "I'd live."

"I don't think they will let me," Violette said.

"Chicot?"

"Yes."

"Why should he want you dead?"

"For one reason," Violette said. "I know him very well, and now I am untrustworthy. Didn't I try to save your life?" She moved her hands slightly, and their slimness and colour caught his eye. "But don't blame yourself; I was already desperate."

"Sackcloth and ashes," murmured the Toff.

"I don't understand you."

"Good girl becomes bad girl, bad girl repents, life looks hopeless, death the way out." His eyes were laughing at her. "Is that it?"

She didn't answer.

"You know, Violette," said Rollison, taking her arm and squeezing her gently, "you've really got much, much more than most sweet young things. Let's deal with Chicot and our problem first, shall we? Your search for Marie, mine for Daphne—and let's deal with dying afterwards, shall we?"

She pulled herself free.

"I don't think you understand," she said. "I come of a very high-born family, and to return would be to the dying shame and great hurt of my parents. For myself——" she shrugged. "For them it is different."

"France is still France," marvelled Rollison, but he wouldn't let her gloom. "Finish this search, and then we'll start on your problem. I'm going to need a lot of help, and most of it will be from you."

She regarded him steadily. The sun beat down upon them, and he felt the effect of its burning on the back of his head, but Violette looked and sounded as cool as she could be in the air-conditioned saloon below deck.

"Why are you an enemy of Chicot?" she asked.

"I don't know him."

"But he knows you," said Violette. "I think one of the reasons why they intend to kill you is that you might find out who he is," she added, with that thoughtful gravity. "There is something you know or you have done which worries him. So——" She shrugged.

"Curtains," murmured the Toff. "They've been ordered before, and somehow didn't fit. Have you a photograph of Chicot?"

"No," she said.

"Where did you stay when you were with him?"

"Sometimes at the Villa, sometimes on board the *Nuit Verte*. This other girl, this Madeleine," went on Violette with a disparaging shrug of her shoulders, "is one of his new friends. She will be missing from home, and the police will look for her. They will not find her. Several times Chicot's yacht has been searched, but nothing has ever been found. Oh, the police suspect."

"What do they suspect?" asked the Toff very softly.

"That the *Nuit Verte* goes across to Algiers and to other North African ports, always with a cargo of girls, perhaps with other things. What do you call it?—the white-slave traffic. Some of these girls want to go; it is exciting, it is enthralling. I believe that is where they disappear to. But Morency and the others are too clever. There is a spy in the *commissariat de police*, who warns them if there is to be a raid. I know that; I have heard them talk of it. So when the *Nuit Verte* or any other boat is searched—it is empty."

"Do you *know* all this?"

"I only guess."

Rollison found it easy to believe her.

They were silent for a few seconds, with the gentle lapping water for company.

Suddenly:

"Violette," said the Toff.

"Yes?"

"There was a little beggar on the promenade this morning. He followed you. His eyes——"

She looked as if she could cry, and he was sure that she knew that the beggar was dead.

"I know," she said. "Sautot saw him, and went to question him. He was frightened, and confessed that he was working for you, that he'd seen this Daphne Myall. Sautot told him to go in front, and——"

"But why *kill*?"

Violette said quietly: "I am not sure, M. Rollison, but I believe that they were terribly afraid you can prove that the English girl has been at the Villa Seblec. That would bring the police, and—they greatly fear that."

"But if the body were found——"

"They would have taken it away. They were going to when I tried to leave the Villa. They stopped me, and began to question me."

"Tell me more about them," invited Rollison.

She told him.

There was Morency, an old Englishman, who seemed to be in charge. Sautot, whom he realised he had shot, a man from the Paris slums who had no scruples. Raoul, whom she hated——

She touched Rollison's arm:

"This is the truth, *m'sieu*. I live with fear. I dare not return to Nice. Sautot or one of the other servants will be searching. They would kill me, before I could get to the police. And how *could* I go to the police? All I have done will be told, all that my sister has done. There would be such shame for my parents." She paused, but obviously hadn't finished, and Rollison waited. "I would prefer to die," she said at last.

He was sure that she meant it.

He could tell her that there would be greater shame in letting such men as Chicot, Sautot, Morency, and Raoul go unpunished, free to plunder and kill and spoil.

Telling her that could wait.

"We'll swim ashore when we're closer in," said Rollison, "and wade to the beach among the other bathers. They'll be there in their hundreds. Afterwards we'll find a spot for you to hide. Game?"

"Game?"

"Willing?"

She was silent; but her eyes began to glow as with hope.

"Yes," she said at last. "But I should wait a little while," she advised. "You look as if you are too hot already, and you have been standing for a long time in the sun. If we rest in the saloon first, it will be better."

"Oh, we're not quite ready to go yet," agreed the Toff. So she had common sense and a cool head, to help her in her fears for her sister and herself; and of the police.

He wondered if there was a reason for her fear of the police which she hadn't told him.

They turned away, and walked over the hot deck into the welcome coolness of the staircase.

"Is there any medical kit on board?" Rollison asked.

"Oh, yes, always. Dr. Morency keeps one case here."

"He's a real doctor?"

"Yes. Of all the men I have met while serving Chicot," announced Violette, "I like Dr. Morency less than any of them. He is so weak, so frail, so smooth, so gentle, so—*evil*." She spat the word out. "I change my mind. Dr. Morency first, Raoul after him, then——" She shrugged. "Why do you want the doctor's equipment?"

"I'd like to send Raoul to sleep for a little while," Rollison told her solemnly.

She looked at him, but didn't ask why.

She was quite a remarkable woman.

.   .   .   .   .

Rollison looked about, to make sure no other craft was near, before going below to search for the medical kit. It was in one of the sleeping-cabins, built into the wall. Most of the dozens of phials of drugs meant nothing to him, but they told him that the cruiser often travelled to far places; drugs for most emergencies were here. There was also a small surgical kit, the kind carried on cargo-ships which had no doctor on board.

He found a hypodermic syringe, and morphia. He was knowledgeable about morphia, its doses and its possible effects. He filled a fine needle, loaded the hypo, and, followed by Violette, went into the sleeping-cabin where the two prisoners lay. Both were awake, staring towards the door; Raoul seemed to be in greater fear than Gérard.

"What—what are you going to do?" croaked Raoul. "You cannot leave us here. We——"

"Prefer to feed the fishes?" asked Rollison, with mock ferocity. "You keep quiet. Violette," he added to the girl, "we'll do Gérard first. Roll up his sleeve."

Gérard winched.

"*What are you going to do?*" cried Raoul.

"I haven't quite decided," said the Toff. "We're going ashore, and I can't risk you shouting for help, even if you dare. So I'm going to put the pair of you to sleep. Whether you wake up again depends on what I feel like later."

Raoul bit on a scream.

Gérard, tight-lipped, stared at Violette. She undid the button at his left sleeve and pulled it up. Rollison stood close to the bunk. He looked into Gérard's face, and winked; and put a finger to his lips. Gérard gaped. He made a play of stabbing the needle into the strong, tanned arm, and then drawing it out; and he gasped and grunted, as Gérard might do.

"That's one finished," he said, and bent down to Raoul. "Now you."

Raoul's arm was already bare, and Rollison plunged the needle in. Raoul winced, but there was a difference in his expression. It was as if he had resigned himself to what was happening and knew that pleading would not help. Now, he hated. Rollison saw that in his eyes; saw the way he looked at Violette, and understood what she meant when she said that he was bad.

If Raoul had his way with Violette——

Rollison said: "All right, we'll leave them." He went to the door. Violette stepped out; he followed and stood close to it. The door was closed, but he could hear the creaking as one of them tried to turn on his bunk.

Raoul began to swear . . .

Gérard didn't speak.

Raoul fell quiet in ten minutes, perhaps a little less. If Rollison had judged the dose aright, he would be out for at least two hours, almost as dead as a dead man. So Rollison opened the door again, and Violette followed him in. She had not asked a question about what he intended to do.

She had been trained in a hard school.

Gérard's eyes, blue and bright, were turned towards the door. He was sweating, for it was hot in the airless cabin. He licked his lips, and Rollison turned to Violette.

"Will you get him a drink?"

"At once," she said, and went off.

"All right, Gérard," Rollison said to the lad; "I'm not going to hurt you, yet. Violette's wised me up to the general situation. I know about Madeleine." He didn't say that he wondered how Madeleine had allowed herself to marry Raoul, or what irresistible pressures had been exerted against him and his sister. "You've half a chance to get Madeleine and yourself out of the jam. Do you want to?"

"Do—do I *want* to——" Gérard's voice was cracked. "How?"

"Wait a minute," Rollison said.

Violette came in, carrying a long glass of lemon squash, with ice chinking against the glass. Rollison helped Gérard to sit up, and Violette put the glass to his lips. She was as aloof as a nurse.

Gérard gulped, gasped, drained the glass to the bottom, then lay back against Rollison's arm, gasping for breath.

"Next time take it easier," advised Rollison. He offered a cigarette, and Gérard nodded vigorously. He lit it for the youth, then lit one for Violette and himself. He stalled for several minutes, until Gérard looked much more himself, a fresh-faced boy. Then he said quietly: "What would happen if you turned against Chicot, Gérard?"

The answer came as swiftly as Gérard could speak.

"He would kill me."

"And Madeleine?"

"I do not know what he would do to Madeleine," said Gérard very quietly, "but I know what he would do to most girls. He would send them away."

"Where to?"

Gérard said: "Some to Algiers, I know. Others——" He shrugged. "They are at the Villa. I go to bed; next morning they are gone. I do not know where."

"Have you seen an English girl named Myall—Daphne Myall?"

"No," answered Gérard; "but I do not always know the name, and sometimes they are at the Villa for only a few hours."

"Does Raoul know more than you?"

"It is probable," Gérard confessed. "I know very little."

"Will he help Madeleine?"

"He would do nothing to help her if it is against Chicot," Gérard said. "I think that is why I hate him so much."

"Gérard," said Rollison quietly, "I'm going to leave you and Raoul on board, anchored out here. Sooner or later Chicot's friends will come and take over. You'll be unconscious, or just coming round, when they arrive. Raoul will think that you lost consciousness before he did. He won't know about this conversation, won't know that I'm making a proposition which might help to save both you and Madeleine."

Gérard said between clenched teeth: "What is it?"

"Go back to the Villa with them, and try to find out two things. Why they suddenly decided to kill me, and where they sent the English girl, Daphne Myall. Daphne Myall," Rollison repeated, allowing the English name time to register on Gérard's mind. "Will you do that, Gerard?"

"And if I do?"

"If you do, and if we can find evidence to put Chicot in court, you'll be protected," Rollison promised. "And once you get us the information, I'll see that you and Madeleine are taken away, out of their reach."

"*Can* you do that?"

"Yes," said Rollison firmly, "I can do that, Gérard." He went on briskly: "Do you know the Café Lippe?"

"In the Rue de Sauvant, behind the Hotel San Roman?"

"Yes. Take messages there. Leave them with the *patron*, Papa Lippe himself; say they are for the agent for M. Rambeau. He'll pass them on. If you write anything, use block capitals so that your handwriting can't be recognised."

Gérard said: "Yes, yes. If I fail——" He shrugged, touched with the same fatalism as Violette. "It can be no worse than it is," he said. "I will try. Why do they wish to kill you, and where did they send this Daff-nee My-all?"

"That's right," said the Toff. "And now I'm going to give you a shot that will put you to sleep. It won't hurt; just relax."

Gérard said: "I will try, *m'sieu.*"

·   ·   ·   ·   ·

It was four o'clock.

No other craft had approached nearer than five hundred yards, but soon they would be among the craft in the bay.

On deck it was hotter than it had been—the first slight cooling breeze of evening had not yet touched the water. Nice seemed a long way off, and was visible through a faint haze. Heat shimmered off the deck and the roof of the engine-house and the cabin. Rollison, on deck alone, scanned the sea in all directions, and saw no craft approaching. Chichot's men would probably wait until dark before coming out, now that they had waited so long. The police-search for the other cabin cruiser probably explained why there had been no chase; no one at the Villa Seblec wanted to clash with the police, yet they would know there was trouble on board the *Maria*. Whatever it was, they would leave here soon. He didn't want to take the *Maria* in too far: just far enough for them to be able to swim ashore.

They could use the dinghy for a mile or so, and leave the cabin cruiser anchored here.

He went towards the stern, and the spot where he had climbed aboard, and as he did so, saw the unbelievable. It was there in front of his eyes, but he didn't believe it at first.

.   .   .   .   .

A hand gripped the deck.

10

THE FAITHFUL CLOWN

ROLLISON crept closer to the rails. The hand, more brown than white, gripped firmly. The ends of the fingers were flat and broad, and the half-moons had a yellowish tinge. He heard a new sound, a louder lapping of the water against the side of the *Maria*. The breeze, springing up suddenly, might be the reason for that, for it would first be noticed on the water.

A man, swimming, might also cause it.

Rollison went down on his stomach when he was close to the rail. The dark hand was several yards to his right. He inched himself forward, then peered over the side. There was imminent danger of being seen, but he needed only a second to judge the extent of the danger.

He saw one man, holding on to the deck; another, climbing up the rope which he himself had climbed; a third, standing in the dinghy, which was swaying to and fro, and causing the splashing sounds. The silence with which the three men moved was menace in itself. Obviously two of them planned to swing themselves over the side at once; they might then wait until the third was aboard.

Rollison slithered away, got slowly to his feet, crouched low, and scurried towards the stairway. A picture of the three men was as vivid as a photograph in his mind's eye. Brown, wet bodies, dark loin-cloths, sharp features and big, bare feet; these men were Arabs from the other side of the Mediterranean, powerful swimmers, men to whom life was cheap. The rippling muscles of the man climbing the rope told of great physical strength. No craft was in sight, so they had swum from one a long way off.

Rollison reached the head of the stairs, peered over the top of the engine-house, and saw the hand; nothing else.

He went half-way down.

"*Violette!*"

She must have been waiting for a call, because she appeared from the saloon at once. The beach dress was gone. She wore a comparatively decorous swim-suit, and moved with cat-like grace that could take the Toff's mind off most things, but not off the three brown men.

He whispered:

"Hurry, we're being boarded."

He turned and led the way.

The hand was still there, and another had joined it; that was what the brown-skinned men meant to do: wait there until all three could swing aboard at the same time, then make a rush for the cabins.

They might come at any moment.

"Up forrard," he whispered, and took Violette's hand. He swung towards the bows, bare feet making more noise than he liked, although Violette did not make a sound. "Three Arabs," he told her, and he felt her muscles go taut, the sinews tighten. "We'll be all right. Swing over the bows and drop into the water. Make as little noise as you can."

"All right," she whispered, and he let her go.

He turned, to look at the stern. The rail he meant to climb was two yards away; just two steps. Once he was over it would not matter if the brown men came aboard or not. He could not have moved more swiftly, and only a second was left; the second seemed an agonising time. He reached the rail and swung himself over. For a flash of time he was facing the stern, hands on the rail ready to lower himself to the deck and then to drop.

He heard Violette cleave the water with a gentle *swiiiiish* of sound.

Then the three men came aboard almost in one movement, lithe bodies stretched up, hands clutching the rails, ready to vault. They must have boarded ships like this a hundred times; it was over before Rollison could take his hands off the rails.

That was not all. He saw the knives in their mouths, all three glistening in the sun. The sharp, pointed blades were nearly a foot long.

The men were staring towards the engine-house, not the stern.

Rollison dropped down to the sea. He didn't know whether a man glanced towards him and he had been seen. He kept his body stiff, his toes pointing downwards, until his feet and his legs were almost in one straight line. He went in, and deeply under. Water closed silently about him. He seemed to be going down for a long time, before he began to strike out for the surface.

When he reached it, the three men might be waiting with knives poised.

He gritted his teeth as he shot up out of the water, took one deep breath, and plunged under again. But saving himself wasn't the only thing: there was Violette, who might not know the men were already aboard.

He broke the surface, dashed the hair and water out of his eyes, and turned on to his back. The *Maria* was already twenty yards away, and the reflection of her white sides shimmered on the water.

The men were not in sight.

He turned his head, and saw Violette. She was twenty yards away and swimming strongly towards him. He turned over on his stomach and swam steadily, letting her catch up with him. They were so close, when she did, that their arms touched.

"Three of them, with knives," he warned her. "Keep under water as much as you can."

"Yes," she promised.

They dived. There was a cleanness about the sea, and a sense of complete mastery which nothing else could give. Rollison kept his eyes closed, swam under water for fully sixteen seconds, then bobbed up. Violette wasn't in sight. He felt a moment of panic, but she appeared only a few feet away, shaking her head vigorously. He glanced round at the cruiser, which was riding the still sea beautifully.

No one was at the rails.

"They're bound to come soon," he said, and wondered if she heard him. "Go as fast as you can."

She nodded.

He took a few strong strokes towards the shore, then dived under again. When he came up he turned over on his back, so that he could see the *Maria*. It was a long way off now: a hundred yards or more. With luck, they wouldn't be seen. He felt almost light-hearted with relief, and when Violette appeared, ten feet ahead of him, he waved, grinned at her, and caught her up.

"Race you!"

"Fifty strokes," she said, and entered into the spirit of it swiftly, feeling the same kind of release from fear as he.

They struck out. After the first few strokes she was a foot ahead, swimming magnificently; Rollison wondered what she would be like if she were fresh. He kept just behind her. He could overtake her if he made an effort, but it would delight her to win; if he were close behind it wouldn't matter. He kept glancing back, wondering why the men didn't appear at the side. They would have been below by now, and found Gérard and Raoul. The first thing they would do, surely, was look over the side to see if anyone was in sight.

He swam on.

.   .   .   .   .

Rollison did not know that two of the men, knives in their mouths, were already in the water, swimming after him and Violette.

.   .   .   .   .

At fifty strokes Violette was an arm's length ahead. She turned on her back with a single, easy movement, and smiled with gaiety good to see. She was as much at home in the water as she would be in a *salon*, in a Rambeau night-club, or in some stately home. He hair had been swept back by the water so that it was quite straight again: that was the best style for her, it threw the beauty of her bone structure into clear prominence.

"Very close," she said. "Did you let me win?"

"I'll beat you next time!"

"We must go steadily now; it is a long way."

"We will," agreed Rollison soberly. He wondered if it would have been wise to try to get into the dinghy. Was 'wise' the word? It would have taken them five minutes, they might have been seen before they were actually free of the *Maria*. Arabs could probably swim twice as fast as he could row a dinghy, even in this smooth sea.

It was warm, soothing, comforting. Nice was so far away that it was almost invisible; just a line of white seen through a haze. They were at least a mile offshore, but they wouldn't have to swim all that way: there were bound to be small craft afloat, between them and the shore. There was a current, Rollison knew, which would take them towards Cap Mirabeau, where the craft of a yachting club were always at anchor.

The warmth of the sea and sun induced a kind of lassitude. It had been a mistake to expend so much energy in that wild burst of speed, but there were two advantages: it had got them further away from the *Maria*, and had worked the excitement out of their systems. It was going to be a long time before he forgot the sight of the three lean, brown men with the knives in their mouths, and their teeth flashing.

Violette had dropped into a long, steady side-stroke; she could swim for miles with it. He did the same. He had almost forgotten to look for the men, for he had given up thought of imminent danger. But he turned over again, not expecting to see a thing, just to make sure.

He saw a dark head appear out of the water, not fifty yards away.

Brown arms and shoulders appeared for a second, then disappeared, as the Arab dived. The sight was so momentary that it was like a mirage. Smooth, blue water with the *Maria* five hundred yards away—the dark head and moving arms—and the smooth water again, with no ripples which Rollison could see.

"*Violette!*" he called with sudden urgency, and immediately she stopped swimming and turned over on her back, kicking her legs to keep afloat. She couldn't see his expression. "One of them is swimming after us. Head for the nearest point, and get in touch with Simon Leclair—ask for his address at the Café Lippe or at the *Baccarat*. Understand?"

She understood.

Fear touched her features as she turned round and started to swim again, those long, devouring strokes which hurtled her through the water. But fast as she went, she wasn't likely to have the speed of the Arab.

Was there only one?

Rollison changed direction slightly, gradually widening the distance between him and Violette; if there were just the one man, he would have to let one of them get away, while he went for the other.

Rollison found it hard to breathe. His teeth were clenched tightly, and he was sick with the sickening thump of his heart. The Arabs were probably expert under-water swimmers, and would be accustomed to using knives—against sharks and octopi, perhaps against men.

He could see Violette, moving beautifully fast.

Then he saw the man bob up in the water, not twenty feet behind her; the sun glistened on the knife the Arab now had between his teeth.

11

THE BATTLE IN THE SEA

ROLLISON did not know if there were another Arab in the water, near. There was the girl and the man behind her, no longer trying to keep under water, but skimming it. Only Violette's speed kept him at bay, but he was catching up on her slowly; in a few minutes he would be close behind. The recollection of the beggar's battered skull told Rollison what would happen then. One slash from that knife would be enough in Violette's smooth body.

He did not see the other man, only a little way from him,

still under water, but with his eyes open, and able to see Rollison's pale body.

The man surfaced, with hardly a sound.

Unaware of him, Rollison struck out towards Violette and the Arab near her. He had never swam with such power or such desperation. Hurling his body through the water, he waited for the moment that would come, to shout a warning.

He closed the gap.

He would not be able to keep the speed up for long, but this one burst would give him and her a chance. There wouldn't be another.

Ten yards . . .

Five yards were between him and the Arab, who was no more than five behind Violette.

Then the Arab turned his head, as if sensing danger. The sun glinted on the knife. His hand moved as he snatched his knife from his teeth, leapt out of the water and plunged under.

Violette, knowing nothing of this, went on.

Rollison had no idea that the second man was only yards behind him. The danger he knew was quite enough. The Arab could see under water and would be coming at him now, knife in hand. He could not slash through the water, his cutting motion would have to be slow and deliberate.

The Toff saw him.

Legs moving, arms cleaving the water, he was a brown streak only a foot or two from the surface, and very close at hand. His chin was up, and he stared at Rollison. Rollison did the only thing he could, and doing it, he felt a strange despair; strange, because he had seldom known it.

He could not beat these men.

On land he'd have a chance; on deck, too; if only he had stayed on board. Instead, he had acted on impulse and thrown his life away.

He jumped up in the water, and then dived, striking out

so that he could plunge as deep as possible. He felt something touch him; an arm. He shivered. He struck out harder, head still towards the bottom, but he could not stay under too long; he would be exhausted when he surfaced.

His speed slackened.

He struck out for the surface and the precious air. He could see the quivering lines of the water; a school of tiny, colourful fish, their tails moving sluggishly—*and two men.*

They were close together, and seemed to be some distance off. Two of them——

He broke surface, and couldn't see them. Panic touched him, for he couldn't see Violette either. Then he caught sight of her, still swimming strongly towards the shore. There was a different sound, too—a kind of rumbling. *Rm-rm-rm-rm-rm-rm.* Was it the water in his ears? He started to swim towards the shore. The Arabs were behind him, and he couldn't be sure that they could see him, but he hadn't much doubt.

Rm-rm-rm-rm-rm-rm.

It was an engine? A motor-launch? Hope leapt. An aeroplane? Yes, that was it. He saw it passing over his head, the sound strangely muted by the water; a small petrol-engined machine which wasn't flying very high. It didn't offer any hope at all. There wasn't any, unless the Arabs gave up; and there was no reason to believe that they'd do that.

Rollison turned on his back, and faced a man only two yards away, knife in hand. The man was diving.

Here it was.

Rollison swung himself round and hurled himself at the spot where the man had been. He saw the lithe brown figure slip beneath him. Agile as a fish, the man would turn in half the time it would take Rollison. He trod water for a few vital seconds, and saw the shape again. Man for man, he would take a chance, but that knife and that expertness

threatened too much. He saw the Arab about to break surface——

And then he had his luck.

The man changed his mind and dived again, coming
straight towards Rollison without knowing exactly where
Rollison was. The end of that first diving movement should
bring him very close—he should break water close by.

Rollison let himself fall forward, and floated easily. He
saw the brown streak, slowing down and very near him. He
saw the knife under the water, the black head, the muscular
shoulders. He thrust his hand down in a snatching movement, his fingers crooked, hoping desperately that he would
strike the wrist close to the knife.

He did.

He felt the bone between his fingers, clutched and twisted.
The hand was so near the surface that he could exert powerful pressure. The man broke surface wildly. Rollison
heard him gasp, heard the bubbly intake of his breath. He
thrust the wrist back savagely and brought a squeal of pain.

The fingers opened, the knife dropped.

Rollison saw it going down slowly, the point showing.
The handle was carrying it down. He felt a hand at his neck;
brown fingers clutched and then slid off his wet skin. He
turned, and butted the Arab in the nose with his forehead.

The man fell back, splashing noisily.

Rollison swung himself round, gasping for breath, knowing that it would take all the strength he had left to reach a
boat. Then he saw the second Arab, only a few yards away,
with the knife in his mouth.

The sense of despair swept over him again.

He couldn't fight, couldn't hope for such luck twice running. Compared with him, the Arab was fresh, and he had
probably seen what had happened and would be out for
blood. Well, here it was. Should he go forward and try to
fight it out, or turn and swim and hope?

He wanted to swim away.

Even then he found himself trying to work out what chance he had. He was actually on the turn, with the brown-skinned man coming towards him very fast, when he saw Violette's head bob up a little to the left of the Arab, and out of his line of vision.

He wanted to shout.

He changed his mind, and trod water, facing the man and slowing him down. The Arab was waiting for a trick; he trod water too, ready to plunge right or left, whichever way Rollison plunged. Violette came up behind him with swift, near-silent strokes.

It was strange to see her golden brown hand close about his neck, and tighten.

The Arab choked.

Rollison plunged towards him.

.   .   .   .

The Arab sank, slowly, his mouth open. The red of blood tinged the blue water. The knife was in Rollison's hand. Some way off, the other Arab was swimming back towards the *Maria*. Violette and Rollison were floating on their backs and side by side, gradually recovering their breath. They hadn't spoken from the moment when Rollison had plunged the knife between the Arab's ribs.

Soon they were breathing normally.

"Better start," said Rollison. "Ready?"

"When you wish."

"One minute," said Rollison.

He felt as if all the strength had been drained out of him.

He wished that he had not killed; it had been one of them or the Arab, but the taking of life had a finality which brought its own horror. Yet with one man dead and the other in flight, he could call it a miracle. But he didn't try to raise a smile, and he sensed that Violette felt much the same as he.

"We'll start now," he said.

The girl turned. They headed for the shore, with the cool waters about them and the sun still warm, although not striking on the backs of their heads. Rollison faced a new danger; or a danger which had been forgotten—the task of swimming so far.

Could Violette?

Could he?

It could not have been ten minutes later that he heard the rumbling sounds of an engine again. This time it was not an aircraft, but a little outboard motor boat with a young couple on board.

.   .   .   .   .

The youngsters were American, fresh, clean-limbed, eager, curious, generous.

"Why, sure, we'll take you ashore, sir. Glad to have the opportunity. How did you come to be swimming out this far?"

"It's two miles offshore, at least," the girl declared.

"Don't exaggerate, honey," said the youth. "It's no more than a mile, but that's plenty. How——"

"There are young fools and old fools," quoth Rollison. He was sitting in the thwarts, with a borrowed white sweater round his shoulders, smoking, Violette sitting close by his side, wearing a pale blue sweater that was wickedly small for her. "We're the middle-aged variety." He grinned at Violette, whose English was not good enough to understand what that implied. "Do you know the Ile de Seblec?"

"Oh, sure, way across there." The youth pointed.

"We challenged ourselves to a swim from the Ile to Cap Mirabeau," said Rollison. "See what I mean by fools?"

"Why, that's eight *miles*!" cried the American. "You swam this far—say, that's what I call swimming, sir! I'd be proud if I could swim as far as that. We'll be glad to take you anywhere you like."

"Cap Mirabeau will do fine," Rollison said; "we've friends near there."

The stuttering noise of the engine was like a lullaby.

Rollison felt tired out, but no worse. He had dropped the knife when he had seen the outboard, and with it, something of the nausea had gone.

Violette's eyes were droopy. The American girl, who had a complexion nearly as dark as the Arabs, and the nicest way of talking, looked at them, marvelling.

The youngsters talked eagerly.

She was Janet Wetherby; he was Slade Mikado, and you didn't have to think of Gilbert and Sullivan or the English Member of Parliament! His father was in textiles, mostly underwear, and you couldn't think of anything more prosaic than that, could you? They were going to be married soon. He'd been sent out here to get a little idea of what the European agencies of Mikado Textiles were like, and Janet was the daughter of the manager of the Paris office. Everything was fine. Europe was fine. The Riviera was fine. The weather was wonderful. They were going to be married in New York, were to fly back in a week from now, and after that he'd have plenty of work to do—his father's health wasn't so good.

Hadn't he seen Mr. Rollison somewhere?

Rollison?

Why, could he be that private eye he'd heard so much about?

.   .   .   .   .

"Mr. Rollison," said Slade Mikado, shaking Rollison's hand vigorously, "I hope you and Miss Monet will come and have dinner with us, and maybe go to a dive afterwards. The *Baccarat's* not bad at all. We're staying at the Royal, if you find you've time——"

"You'll have dinner with us," said Rollison firmly, "but not tonight, if you'll forgive us."

"Any time at all," breezed Slade. "Right now we're going to visit some friends, and tonight wouldn't be so good, anyway."

"You will let us see you again, won't you?" pleaded Janet Wetherby. "You're quite a hero, Mr. Rollison; but I expect you know all about that."

"People talk too much," Rollison said. "You see what really happens when I do try to do something unusual. Yes— we'd hate to let you go back home without seeing you again."

He looked towards the jetties. The largest one at Cap Mirabeau was public, where anyone could call and tie up; and from where a few cabin cruisers took sedentary-minded tourists on trips along the coast. The breeze was coming up now, and boats were moving up and down a little. There was craft of all sizes, from a three-hundred-ton yacht with magnificent lines, to skiffs. There were many people on the jetty, too, but only one whom Rollison recognised.

He grinned, in spite of his mood.

Simon Leclair sat on the side, with his knees doubled up and his long chin resting on them. He wore an old, shapeless white hat, a cigarette drooped from the corner of his mouth, and his eyes were half-closed. His long feet actually overlapped the edges of the jetty, which was very long and freshly painted. Half-way along, two old fishermen in blue blouses and jeans were mending fishing-nets, and looking as if they had all the time in the world.

Slade Mikado nursed the little boat alongside, and a fisherman caught the rope he threw. He helped Violette out; and every man in sight watched her as she moved. She still wore the clinging sweater, and carried herself proudly; yet Rollison knew that she looked round, already frightened of whom might be there to see and to welcome her.

He jumped on to the jetty.

"You're all right here," he said quickly. "Walk along with our two rescuers, and wait for me at the end of the jetty."

She nodded, without arguing.

"I'll catch you up in a couple of jiffs," Rollison said to Slade Mikado.

The Americans and Violette went on, still watched by all the men in sight, while Rollison moved towards the fisherman who had hauled them in and was now tying up the outboard. To do this, Rollison had to pass behind the faithful clown, who hadn't moved at all.

"You saw the girl I brought ashore," he said to the back of Simon's neck.

Simon did not turn round.

"I could also tell you what Fifi would call her." he said.

"She's in acute danger," Rollison told him quietly. "wherever she goes and wherever she is. Take her to a small hotel, and let me know where to find her. Somewhere or someone you can trust with her life, even if a large bribe is offered."

Simon said: "*So.*"

"Will you?"

"Of course."

"I'll tell her to go with you," Rollison said. He appeared to be looking out to sea, for the sight of a sail or a boat he thought was due. "If you're followed, I'll follow you."

He moved away. Simon still sat there, chin close to bony knees. Rollison walked quickly after the young Americans and Violette, who was between them. All the men watched her; and one of them or more than one might work for the man called Chicot.

12

A MESSAGE FROM CHICOT

ROLLISON had a taxi waiting for him. Simon had caught up with them, and was now helping Violette into his ridiculous little bumble-bee of a car, the roof of which was still wide open. The evening breeze was making his red hair wave, and by the side of the little car he looked ridiculous. But he was envied. Any man escorting Violette would be envied. Englishmen, Americans, Swedes and Belgians, Swiss, Italians, and even Frenchmen at their leisure looked at her, and it wasn't only because of her superb carriage. She had a disturbing influence; she even disturbed the Toff.

Simon bent double, and insinuated himself into the car. He slammed the door. When that was done, there seemed to be an audible sigh from fifty pairs of lips. Then he started the engine and drove off.

Rollison sat in a taxi.

Two or three cars were moving along the road from the esplanade at the Cap Mirabeau, but none seemed to follow the midget Renault. Rollison told his taxi-driver to move on, and followed fifty yards behind. A mile further on he felt quite sure that no one was following Violette; and equally sure that no one was following him.

He could relax.

He hadn't any cigarettes, and missed them badly. He could have had a hundred for asking, from Slade Mikado. Slade had driven his Janet off in a purring Buick, the colour of cream from a Jersey cow. They'd gone in the other direction, for they were to call at a villa approached from the Middle Corniche.

Rollison sat back in the car, and was jolted and swayed from side to side. It was warmer ashore than it had been at sea. The evening air wasn't yet really cool, for it was full daylight. The sea was darkening. He closed his eyes, and seemed to see nothing but the blue water and the snaking brown figures. Sitting here, it was hard to believe that it had happened; harder to believe that the threat had been so acute, yet had been beaten off.

He could see a knife, falling, pointing upwards.

He could see blood, discolouring the sea, and the open mouth and the teeth of the Arab who had sunk out of sight.

Soon he was driving along the main promenade. Traffic was much thicker than it had been that morning, the promenade itself was thronged with people taking a stroll before dining at leisure. Everyone seemed to be taking the air. The tassels hanging from the coloured umbrellas and the gay awnings, on the front, at the terraces, and high up on the face of the great hotels, all bobbed gently to and fro in the breeze. Nice was its warm and beautiful self. A dozen *fiacres* were being drawn, a thousand sleek cars purred.

The taxi drew up outside the Hotel San Roman. A porter sprang to open the door, looked startled at Rollison's garb, then beamed upon him.

"Pay the bill, please," Rollison said, and gave a mechanical smile.

"But of course, sir!"

That was easy. It was equally easy to skip across the terrace, where the orchestra was back—dressed in different clothes—to play for dinner and the evening's relaxation. The big foyer was almost deserted, except for Alphonse, who was behind the desk. His eyes widened at the sight of Rollison, his stubby hands were raised.

"*M'sieu*, you walk again!"

"Yes," said Rollison, and summoned up his mechanical smile. "It wasn't so bad, after all. I'm in a hurry, Alphonse. Have there been any messages?"

"But no," said Alphonse. "Unless they are in your room."

He came away from his desk in order to escort M. Rollison to the gate of the lift, and that was a signal honour. A lift-boy, looking corsetted in wine-red and silver buttons, stood nervously on one side. "If the new girl is not satisfactory, *m'sieu*, you will please advise, and we shall arrange for another," Alphonse said.

"New girl?" echoed Rollison.

"The chambermaid, *m'sieu*."

Rollison stopped thinking about a sinking Arab face and a battered skull and a swarm of flies. His voice sharpened.

"Where's Suzanne?"

"It was unfortunate, *m'sieu*," said Alphonse, and spread his hands. "She must have leaned out of the window too far. By good fortune, she did not fall right down to the terrace, but to the main balcony. No one else was there."

They were in the lift; the gates were closed; the old porter, with his silvery hair and silvery beard, had a finger on the button for the third floor. There was the usual clicking sound, and the lift began to climb; it was surely the slowest climbing lift in France.

Horror crept upon the Toff as he said tautly: "What do you mean? Is Suzanne hurt?"

"Hurt?" echoed Alphonse gently. "Yes, badly, *m'sieu*. It is a good thing for her that she died. The doctor said that her injuries were so bad she would not have walked again. It is very sad."

The lift was still crawling up.

The truth came starkly to Rollison, but he did not want to believe it; he rejected it wildly, and his wildness was a measure of his horror.

"What happened?"

"She fell out of the window, *m'sieu*."

"*My* window?"

"But yes," said Alphonse.

Rollison said: "I see," and clamped his teeth together. Soon he went on: "I'm very, very sorry." He pictured the country girl, with the clear skin and the innocent eyes, and he remembered her tales of her home in the valley near Bordeaux; how in the harvest time she went back to the village, but in the season came to earn some money in the fine hotels of Nice. Except for unpleasant men, she had enjoyed every minute of it; and she had had a specially soft spot for him.

"When did it happen?" asked Rollison.

"At a little after one o'clock, *m'sieu.*"

He'd been gone about half an hour, then. Suzanne had helped him to get out of the hotel without being noticed. She had dropped her keys with a thump when danger had threatened, and beckoned eagerly when it had passed. He could see the gleam in her bright eyes, and her astonishment when she saw him in the blue jeans and the jacket.

"The new girl is not very experienced," Alphonse informed him. "You will tell me if she is all right?"

"Yes," said Rollison. "Yes, thanks."

Alphonse, holding his key, went with him to the door, opened it, handed him the key, and went off. If he were puzzled by Rollison's reaction to the news of Suzanne's death, he didn't show it.

Rollison closed the door behind him.

On the table by the side of the one armchair was a tray, with a glass, whisky, and soda; that was how he liked it, and Suzanne had left it for him there. Pain stung his eyes. The unexpectedness of this hurt most; that, and the thought of her innocence, battered and broken as the brown-eyed beggar had been on the rocky cliffs.

Why?

He poured himself a drink, and went to the balcony. The awning was still down, and if Suzanne had been here, she would have seen that it was not, at this hour. He pushed it up, and looked out at the darkening sea and the horizon which seemed to be drawing nearer. A white ship which might be the *Maria* was making its way slowly from headland to headland.

He saw scratches on the stonework of the balcony, perhaps made by Suzanne's shoes.

Why?

Had they broken in to search his room, or to lie in wait for him, and come upon Suzanne, killing to make sure that she could not report that they had been here? Or had they wanted to know where he was?

He felt quite sure that this was to do with Chicot. Chicot was a name, and he hated the name as he had seldom hated in his life.

He looked at the whisky in his glass. A few bubbles from the soda-water were travelling upwards and vanishing in tiny, almost invisible explosions. He tasted the whisky-and-soda gingerly. It seemed all right. He held the glass up, and saw the sediment already settling at the bottom; not much, but enough to be noticeable. He went inside, quickly, and picked up the bottle and carried it, upright and without shaking it, into the better light outside.

There was a filmy sediment.

Poison?

.   .   .   .   .

He sent for another bottle of whisky and syphon of soda, sealed the half-empty bottle with Selotape, and put it back in the wardrobe; he had checked for finger-prints, but all except his own had been wiped off. There would be a nearby chemist who would analyse the contents, and he wouldn't be at ease until he knew the truth.

Any kind of ease seemed a long way off.

The telephone bell rang. He looked at it for a long time, before lifting the receiver.

"Hallo?"

There was a pause, and then Simon Leclair said: "Hallo, friend Toff. Is there more trouble?"

"What makes you think there might be?"

"Your voice, my old friend, but perhaps you are only

thinking of Violette! I will tell you this. I have forgiven you for the trick you played on me, but Fifi has not and will not for a long time. To send me to Cap Mirabeau, when the trouble is elsewhere! Isn't that true?"

"Simon," said Rollison, a little less tensely, "you are a married man, remember, and for some odd reason Fifi loves you. Where's Violette?"

"She is at a little hotel—oh, hotel is too important a name, a little *pension* in Rue de Guy de Maupassant," Simon told him. "Very clean, very good food, very cheap, very nice peoples, very nice *patron*, extra nice neighbours—because we are in the *apartement* next to Violette! I watch, or Fifi watches," declared Simon, "and if she is hurt it is over our dead bodies!"

Rollison didn't answer.

"Toff," said Simon, suddenly anxious. "Are you there? Did you hear? It is nonsense to worry about Fifi; she wants to help as much as I do. Can we forget that it was you who once saved Fifi from much trouble, from years of imprisonment for what she did not do?" He paused, then cried: "*My friend, are you there?*"

"Yes, I'm here," said Rollison, with an effort. "Sorry, Simon. But listen to this. The chambermaid at the hotel was killed this afternoon. The beggar you would not trust was killed this morning. It's only by the grace of God that I came back alive. Don't talk about dead bodies. I wish you hadn't taken Violette to your *pension*. I don't think you were followed, but it's always difficult to be sure."

"We shall be all right," Simon sounded louder, and perhaps a little less confident. "But this is bad. The police——"

"Yes," Rollison said. "Perhaps. Later." He could not ask the police to help Violette, yet. There was Gérard's sister, too; poor Madeleine.

"Be very careful, Simon," Rollison added earnestly. "Let me know what happens, and telephone every hour or so. What's the telephone number of the *pension*?"

Simon told him.

"Thanks," said Rollison. "And remember, be careful."

He rang off.

There was silence until footsteps sounded outside the door; when they stopped, there was a tap. It might be the waiter with the whisky and soda. It might be anyone; friend or enemy. Rollison moved away from the telephone, and went across to the door. He heard the clink of keys; that might be done deliberately, to fool him.

He opened the door, kept his foot against it, peered out, and made sure that the man carried a tray with a bottle and a syphon on it. He opened the door wider, and the man came in. No one else appeared to be in the passage beyond.

"Where you like it, sir?"

"On that table, please."

"Very good, sir." The man was small, dark-haired, boasting a little black line of moustache. He had quick, jerky movements and very little polish. "That is all, sir?"

"Yes, thanks," Rollison said.

The waiter went out, and the door closed with a snap.

Rollison poured himself out another whisky and soda. There hadn't been time to fiddle with these bottles, and there was no sign of sediment on the bottom of either. He needed the drink badly. Suzanne had superseded the pictures of the others; it was a nightmare. He could go to the window and look out and see the balcony, five floors below, on which she had smashed her pretty little body.

The telephone bell rang again.

He moved towards it, half fearfully, took himself to task, yet understood what was happening to him. He was suffering from an accumulation of shock, and a form of exhaustion. He would never know how much the fight in the sea had taken out of him. And now he knew that Chicot might strike anywhere in any way. Nothing and no one was really safe—least of all the man whom many knew as the Toff.

He took off the receiver. "Hallo?"

D

A man asked: "Is that M. Richard Rollison?"

"Yes."

"Good evening," said the man, in a suave, not unpleasant voice. "I wonder if we might have the mutual pleasure of dining together. I am now in the foyer of your hotel, and we could dine there or—if you prefer it—at a restaurant of your own choosing." He did not give Rollison time to comment, just paused slightly, to change the subject, and went on: "We have not met, but we have some common interests. I am a friend of M. Chicot."

13

M. CHICOT?

'I AM a friend of M. Chicot' came out with a blandness which even shook the Toff, who did not reply at once. The speaker seemed to expect a startled silence, for he did not go on. Most men would have asked if Rollison were still there, or would have started fidgeting; not the man who called himself a friend of Chicot.

"I think it had better be here," said Rollison at last. "The chef is reasonable." He paused. "If you like any special dish, I'll ask him to prepare it."

It was the man who called himself a friend of Chicot's time to pause; when he broke the silence, it was with a chuckle.

"I think I shall enjoy meeting you, M. Rollison. By all means, then, at the San Roman. I gladly leave the selection of a meal to you."

"And wines?"

"Naturally."

"And whisky?" asked Rollison, with gentle sarcasm.

The man startled him again, by laughing on a low-pitched note, as if the remark really amused him.

"Very funny," murmured the Toff. "I shall have to introduce some belladonna into the meal tonight. Shall we say eight o'clock?"

"Eight o'clock," agreed the other blandly. "I shall look forward very much to meeting you. I should tell you my name—M. Blanc."

"In England," murmured the Toff, "it would doubtless be Mr. Smith."

'M. Blanc' chuckled and rang off.

"Well, well," murmured Rollison, and put down the receiver slowly. He glanced at a travelling clock on the dressing-table; it was twenty minutes to seven. He smoothed down his hair, finished the whisky, locked the door, and went into the bathroom. He had a cold shower and a brisk rub down, and felt much better.

By then his mood was different; harder.

Until this morning he had been looking for a silly girl —well, a foolish girl—who was known to have been hypnotised by the glamour of the Côte d'Azur. There had been mystery, but not murder. Now two people had died violent deaths, chiefly—well, partly—because they had known and tried to help him. And obviously there were many girls who were in the same plight as Daphne Myall.

They put a heavy burden on his conscience.

Raoul had tried to kill him, while the three Arab swimmers had not brought those knives for the sake of making pretty patterns on the deck. After these failures—poison. Swift as the coming of dawn, the tempo and the gravity of this case had changed.

Why?

What had he learned, to worry Chicot and others so much? He let the question simmer in his mind, put in a call to his London flat, and then began to dress. Suddenly there were a great many things to do, and little time to do them in. M. Blanc intrigued him; but M. Blanc, whether a friend of Chicot or not, was almost certainly trying to distract him; to stop him from doing all that he needed to do.

He drew on the thin black trousers of his dinner-suit at seven-twenty-five precisely. He sat on the side of the bed and called Simon Leclair's number, already beginning to worry because Simon hadn't come through.

A woman answered. While she went to fetch M. Leclair, Rollison was seeing the clown's big face, not red with grease-paint but with blood. . . .

The picture vanished.

"Hallo, Toff!"

"In the life," said the Toff, with great relief. "Simon, I thought you'd decided to desert Nice and go back to Paris. Everything all right?"

"The *pension* is not being watched."

"Good. Two things to do, then. First, collect a bottle from Alphonse at the desk here, and get a chemist to analyse the contents, will you? I don't like the look of the powder at the bottom."

After a short pause, Simon said: "It is truly a wicked business, my friend. Yes, I shall do that."

"And then try to find a way of getting Violette here," said Rollison. "Disguise her any way you can to make sure she can't be recognised, and have her walk through the dining-room at about half-past eight. Can you?"

"It will be dangerous, perhaps."

"Not if she's properly disguised. I'll be dining with a Frenchman, and I want to know if his name is Blanc or if Violette knows him by any other name."

"If it can be done, we will do it," Simon promised.

When Rollison rang off, he lit another cigarette and allowed himself five minutes' complete relaxation, leaning on the big square pillow and looking out of the window at the stars. The night was calm, the wind had dropped, the stars looked close and friendly. They gazed upon life and death, alike, and kept their secrets.

The telephone bell rang.

"M. Rollison, your call to London . . ."

"Thank you," said Rollison, and found himself smiling, because of the man at the other end of the line. It was the man he wished could be here with him, who in a way was his almost perfect foil: Jolly, his general factotum, secretary, butler, chef, and friend. Since heavy losses on the stock markets had compelled the Toff to accept fees for his services, Jolly had also become a kind of business manager; it was he who always quoted fees.

Jolly's voice came as clearly as if he were in this room. He would be standing by the telephone, probably wearing a green baize apron over black trousers, black waistcoat, and white shirt. His lined face would be set gravely, and his brown eyes would be rather doleful, because all that was part of Jolly. It might have started as pose, but it had become factual.

"Hallo, Jolly," greeted Rollison. "Bearing up?"

"Good evening, sir," said Jolly. "I hope I didn't keep you waiting."

"Not a split second. How are you and how are things?"

"There has been no particular deviation from the average norm," asserted Jolly, and accompanying that remark there might be the slightest of smiles in his eyes. "Two possible commissions came in by the morning post, but there is nothing urgent about either of them. Mr. Myall called this afternoon."

"Ah," said Rollison. "The same story?"

"Quite honestly, sir," said Jolly, sounding more human, "my impression was that he is absolutely desperate. Apparently Mrs. Myall feels partly responsible for her daughter's—ah—defection. I think we shall find that Mrs. Myall was extremely censorious and in fact lit the spark which finally sent her daughter away. Mr. Myall says that he is seriously worried about his wife's mental health. I advised him to allow Sir Courtney Laverson to examine her, knowing that Sir Courtney is excellent in all mental sicknesses believed to be due to shock and a sense of guilt."

"Yes," said Rollison. "Good."

"And that's everything, sir."

"Nearly everything," said Rollison, slowly and very thoughtfully. "Something's happened in the past twenty-four hours or so to quicken the pace over here. They're getting homicidal."

"Getting *what*, sir?"

"Homicidal."

"I'm extremely sorry to hear that," said Jolly, "I hoped that you would be having a rest, and—are you *hurt*?" That was the first time his voice sharpened.

"No, but others have been. Try to think of anything that we might have discovered in the past twenty-four hours. Some new factor might explain it. It could have sprung from something you've been up to over there."

There was a long pause.

"I don't think that is very likely," said Jolly at last. "I have been able to do very little. I was in touch again with M. Rambeau, to make sure that it was still in order for you to act as his agent." He paused. "There is perhaps one thing——"

Rollison was sharp: "Yes?"

"He said that he was a little worried about the owner of the *Baccarat* Club in Nice. That is a night-club, of course, but there is also a gaming-room. It is very exclusive, and apparently the proprietor has been protesting to M. Rambeau about his intention to open a cabaret also in Nice. That project has become more imminent, of course, because you have been acting as M. Rambeau's agent. You know what M. Rambeau is like, sir, rather—ah—explosively excitable, and in this matter he was extremely angry. I—ah—got the impression that he resented the interference from M. le Comte de Vignolles——"

"Who?"

"M. le Comte de Vignolles," repeated Jolly firmly. "M. le Comte is the owner of the *Baccarat* Club, although the manager is often represented as the proprietor. I don't wish to labour this point at all, but it had obviously made a deep impression on M. Rambeau. He did not appear to understand why there should be any protest about competition, and I gathered—perhaps that is too strong a word, I had a vague impression that M. le Comte had attempted to threaten M. Rambeau."

"Well, well," murmured the Toff. "To draw me off?"

"In a way, sir, yes. Until you broached the subject, I hadn't seen it quite like that. I am aware that you cannot judge a French gentleman by English reactions, of course. The excitability is a little strange to me, and when it is allied to a member of the theatrical profession, then——"

"I know what you mean," interrupted Rollison. "Did Rambeau say anything else?"

"Apparently it was to be war to the knife," Jolly told him, using the *cliché* without hesitation. "M. le Comte said that he would plan to employ the highest-paid artistes in France at the *Baccarat* and—well, frankly, sir, I assumed that this was a kind of professional jealousy. With it heavy on his mind, M. Rambeau took the opportunity of talking to me about it. Also, he wanted to know how long you would be, and if you were being successful. I took the liberty of telling him again that you were on the—ah, point of success."

"I wish I were. Did that soothe him?"

"I had the distinct impression that when he rang off—the telephone conversation lasted twenty-seven minutes, precisely—he was less troubled."

"Soothing syrup from Jolly! Thanks. Spell Vignolles."

"V–i–g–n–o–l–l–e–s," spelt Jolly.

"Thanks again. Find an excuse for talking to Rambeau in the morning, will you?"

"I will, sir."

"Fine," said Rollison, and smiled as if his man were actually in the room. "Good night."

"Good night, sir," said Jolly, and added after a pause: "You will be very careful, won't you?"

"Very careful indeed," promised Rollison.

And he meant it.

He got slowly off the bed. It was twenty minutes to eight, and he would soon have to go downstairs.

Ninety-nine times out of a hundred he would have thought nothing of this meeting more than he had already. Now it was very different. He could imagine brown-skinned men leaping over the rails of the *Maria*; and he could imagine brown-skinned men climbing up the balconies of the San Roman, until they reached his room. By night, that would be comparatively easy.

He could imagine them lurking at the corners of the passages; or outside his door; or even in the lift.

He would have felt better had he been armed, but his automatic was either tucked in his shoe on the little beach near the Villa Seblec, or had been found by some of the men of the Villa and taken away. Probably it was there. He missed it, but there was one compensation—a curious little gadget which, oddly enough, had been presented to him by a Frenchman. The presentation had not been wholly voluntary, but it had been useful.

It was a beautiful piece of mechanism, and its deadliness was the greater because it looked so innocent. There might be fifty or a hundred cigarette-lighters in the dining-room of the San Roman that evening, but only one which was also a lethal weapon. The tiny bullets which this lighter fired could kill a man if they hit the right spot.

Rollison had an identical lighter, in a different pocket.

He dressed, slipped the two lighters into the respective pockets, and examined himself in the mirror. His white tuxedo fitted as only Saville Row could fit, and within reason, he was satisfied. The real trouble was with the reflections of people who were not there. A dying Arab, sinking through the crystal-clear water. A brown-eyed beggar with a soft voice, who had died while keeping his word. A swarm of flies. And Violette. What was there about Violette? That queenly pride, the almost boastful way in which she flaunted her body, yet was as natural as nature itself could be.

Was it asking for trouble to bring her here tonight?

Simon would not do it unless he felt confident that it could be safely done. He would overrule any decision which the Toff made; would try, but wouldn't take wild chances. Yet it was important to find out the true identity of the man who had telephoned him.

It might be vital.

At five minutes to eight, Rollison left the room.

He had his right hand in his pocket, about the little cigarette-lighter. The fact that he felt so tense was an indication of the seriousness with which he took the threat. He watched the corners. He watched the open ironwork sides of the lift. He watched as he crawled past each of the four floors, alone in the lift but for a page-boy.

Suzanne had been hurled to her death, and the murderers might still be in the hotel.

Nothing happened.

He smiled at the lift-boy, and stepped into the foyer. Two or three people whom he knew slightly were there, but no one who might be M. Blanc. Alphonse was busy at the desk, but made an excuse to free himself when he saw Rollison approach. Rollison gave him the bottle, and told him that a messenger would come for it.

"Yes, *m'sieu*?"

"And if I get a message, have it sent into the dinning-room at once, will you?"

"But of course, *m'sieu*. Will you be dining alone?"

"I hope not," said the Toff, and then sadly shook his head. "And I don't mean what you mean, Alphonse! I am expecting a M. Blanc. Do you know him?"

"Blanc?" echoed Alphonse, wrinkling his lined forehead with outward solemnity. "No, *m'sieu*, the name is not familiar *here*. There was a famous cabaret artiste of great size, you understand, who called himself Mont Blanc—a joke, *m'sieu*—but I understand he drank too much English whisky!" Alphonse looked round the foyer, and saw another man come in. "I recognise everyone who is here, including M. le Comte de Vignolles. It is not often that he honours us."

There was a subtle change in Alphonse's manner.

There was an uneasy feeling in Rollison; for this was almost too much for coincidence.

Obviously the Comte de Vignolles was the man who had just come in. It was obvious at the first glance that he was used to beingf awned upon; that he expected the obsequious attentions of two porters and a small boy, who took his hat, his stick, and his white gloves. As he stripped these gloves off, he looked round the foyer as if seeking someone whom he would recognise.

His gaze fell upon Rollison.

He looked hard at Rollison, smiled faintly, and came towards him. He was tall, elegantly dressed in a dinner-jacket of a deep purple colour, and smoked a cigarette in a long holder. He was the Frenchman of half a century ago, and unquestionably he had something. Vitality? Personality? Whatever it was, no one could mistake it.

He stopped a yard from Rollison. Alphonse did something which Rollison had never known him do before: he bowed low, and spread his hands.

"M. le Comte," he murmured, "what is your pleasure?"

M. le Comte de Vignolles ignored him, and smiled at Rollison.

"I think we are to dine together," he said. "You will know me as M. Blanc."

"M. *Blanc*," breathed Alphonse.

14

M. LE COMTE DE VIGNOLLES

THEY went straight into dinner.

It was like being with royalty. Alphonse and two myrmi-
dons went as far as the door of the cocktail bar; Alphonse
and two minor waiters went as far as the dining-room.
There, the ceremony of recognition and welcome took place
with complete disregard of the fact that at least eight people
were waiting for attention from the head waiter. This was
Jules, with waxed moustaches and a small waxed beard, for
the San Roman believed in giving its clients all the atmosphere
it could. Jules bowed very low indeed. Two other waiters,
his chief deputies, stood by, just slightly relaxed from attention. Two lesser men stood waiting upon them. The guests
who were waiting were so taken by this performance that no
one appeared to be even slightly impatient.

M. le Comte de Vignolles not only looked and acted the
part of a prince; he seemed to live it. There was the proper
carelessness in his manner, as he leant an ear to the platitudinous courtesies of the head waiter, a kind of half-hearted
attention, as if he knew that he must be polite but really, it
was so wearying. He took it all for granted, and for a few
seconds he seemed to forget that the Toff was there.

The Toff walked meekly by his side.

The best table in the room was laid for four people. A
reserved ticket was on it, but was whisked away by one of
the underlings. It was near the terrace, overlooking the
promenade gay with fairy-lights, near enough to hear but not
too close to the patient orchestra; and a space was cleared, so
there were no tables or people to obstruct the view.

Chairs were drawn back in readiness. . . .

A stir of movement switched attention towards the other

end of the huge dining-room. It was the head chef, complete with white stove-pipe hat, his apron stained with juices, followed by three members of his staff. . . .

After fifteen minutes, during which the venerable wine waiter was also brought into the conference, the acolytes withdrew. During the whole performance, Rollison's opinion had been invited and even considered, but as often as not rejected. It was done with utmost suavity. He was not left out, but M. le Comte made it quite clear that he was not of very great importance; that was the one mistake he made.

He attempted to put it right with a broad smile.

"Now, M. Rollison, we can enjoy each other's company! I would have invited you to my home, where there would be less formality, but I was persuaded that you were not likely to accept the invitation."

"From M. le Comte de Vignolles, yes," said Rollison mildly. "From M. Blanc, the friend of M. Chicot——"

"My joke," declared M. le Comte genially. "Sometimes, when I am incognito, I use the name. You like it?"

"The name's all right, but I don't like the company you keep," said Rollison. "The M. Chicot I know about has a shocking reputation." He looked into M. le Comte's mocking eyes, and decided that he did not greatly like this exquisite who had made himself such a reputation. He did not like being made a fool of either, and de Vignolles was trying to do exactly that. "Perhaps you've chosen a dangerous friend, M. le Comte."

"Oh, a little danger," said de Vignolles carelessly. "Would you have the world without any? M. Rollison, I was very anxious to have a talk with you, and I think this is the best way. From now on you will be held in very high esteem by everyone who matters in Nice. This is only the third time in a year that I have entertained a guest in public. When I do, it is to show the world that I expect him to be treated with the utmost courtesy. And I am sure that you will be."

"They weren't exactly brusque before."

"From now on you will find it *very* different," de Vignolles assured him airily. "You will be allowed to go wherever you wish, your command will be law. You might even be welcome at the Villa Seblec, M. Rollison, provided you go to the front door! But that is one thing I cannot promise you. My friendship with M. Chicot is somewhat strained. In fact, we are not friends, but I felt that the use of the word would intrigue you."

"I am intrigued," said Rollison dryly.

"I am delighted," said de Vignolles. "Let me be honest, M. Rollison. I have had many artistes at the *Baccarat*, a night-club of which you may have heard." He paused.

"Vaguely," murmured the Toff.

If de Vignolles sparked, it would betray a pompous conceit. If he smiled——

He laughed, off-handedly.

"Your joke, *m'sieu!* Let me continue. I have the Villa Seblec watched, and I have discovered that M. Chicot has found it displeasing to be annoyed by you. Chicot is a strange fellow. He is a good friend, I am told, but a very bad enemy. He does not always behave in a way which we admire, but I have good reason to be wary of him. I also like the English, and I do not want you to run into trouble here in Nice. So I hope that by this meeting we might solve your problems, M. Rollison, so that you could stay in Nice for as long as you felt inclined, relaxing and enjoying yourself. I need not say that I shall be happy to provide everything you need for relaxation. *Everything*." The mocking glint shone in his eyes again. "Especially if you find a way to—ah—harass our friends at the Villa Seblec."

Rollison said sharply: "Why do you want to cut Chicot's throat?"

"So crude," murmured de Vignolles. "So English! I have told you a little. I have of course heard of your fame. It would please me to see the Villa Seblec change hands, and

Chicot dead. It would be worth a large sum of money to me, M. Rollison."

Rollison said stonily: "How large?"

"Shall we say a million francs? Or one thousand English pounds, *m'sieu*."

"And I have to kill Chicot to earn it?"

De Vignolles said: "His death would be most welcome."

"What harm does he do you?" Rollison asked abruptly.

"Too much," answered de Vignolles.

He saw a waiter approaching, and leaned back. Four waiters came in all, with snails for M. le Comte and oysters for the Toff; and the etceteras. Serving was another ceremony. Rollison looked about him, and saw a flower-girl moving towards them. Something about the way she moved attracted his attention. At first he didn't know what it was. She was taller than most Frenchwomen, and had corn-coloured hair drawn tightly back from her forehead, and she wore a tiny mask. The San Roman like to titillate the curiosity of its clients that way; the flower-girls and the cigarette-girls were always either over-dressed or under-dressed. This girl wore a cloak which concealed her figure, but when the cloak opened as she handed out her wares, it showed that she had plenty to conceal.

She looked at him.

Those eyes were the eyes of Violette.

He smiled at her faintly. She did not let her gaze linger on him for long, but turned to the Comte de Vignolles, and caught his eye. He looked at her dispassionately, and then looked away. She moved on, to nearby tables. Rollison did not watch her, but noticed when she slipped out of the dining-room into the foyer.

The oysters were the best obtainable; from Whitstable.

The snails, obviously, were from Auxerre, and as obviously the Count relished them.

A waiter brought a message for the Toff; just a folded slip of paper. He opened it, and read:

"It is the Count de Vignolles."

He crumpled it up and put it in his pocket, aware that de Vignolles was watching him. He didn't speak. This man was the man who was kicking up a fuss with Rambeau about the rival night-club coming to Nice. This was a man frightened of Chicot, if he could be believed.

Could he?

There was a sole baked in a wine and mushroom sauce which must have been made in the kitchens of Valhalla.

There was venison. . . .

There was roast duck so delicious that it deserved to be regarded as food for the gods.

The wines were perfect.

Two beautiful baskets of fruit and two silver finger-bowls were placed on the table.

"Undoubtedly they try to do well here," said de Vignolles carelessly. "Some grapes, M. Rollison?"

"Thank you," said Rollison, and snipped off a small bunch which were brushed with the lustre of the vine. "They do very well. I still want to know why you want Chicot dead."

"That is my business, *m'sieu*," de Vignolles said. "I do not like what happens at the Villa Seblec."

"What *does* happen?"

"Beautiful girls, who belong to my cabaret, go there and vanish, *m'sieu*. I cannot complain to the police, for they can go where they wish, but I think that this Chicot steals them to make it difficult at the *Baccarat*. Always, new girls in the act, always—but you understand?"

"Remember Daphne Myall?" asked Rollison abruptly.

"The English girl," murmured the Count. "Yes, *m'sieu*, she was exceptionally attractive."

"First, I'm here to find her," Rollison said, with great deliberation. "I intend to take her back to England with me. Second, I like men for their worth, not for their social standing, their money, or their influence. I liked the little man, Gaston, whose head cracked like an egg-shell in the grounds of the Villa Seblec. I also liked Suzanne, the chambermaid here. She was a pretty little thing with a young, pure body, more girl than woman. So two lives wait for avenging. Two people, foully murdered by friends of Chicot. I expect to live to see his head roll from the guillotine, but not to earn your million francs."

De Vignolles said sharply: "What are you saying?"

"That I don't kill for any man," said the Toff coldly. "But if it is any consolation, if I find Chicot and it looks as if he'll cheat the law, I am prepared to kill him with my two bare hands."

He did not smile.

He knew that even de Vignolles would be impressed by that display of feeling, and perhaps be more ready to talk. There was so much to suspect about de Vignolles, too; if Chicot wanted to find out how much the Toff knew, what better way than to send a man who professed hatred?

De Vignolles had plenty to think about, whatever his motives.

Rollison pushed his chair back, stood up, bowed distantly, and walked away. Everyone in the room stared at him, including de Vignolles. Most mouths gaped. Only after the first shock did the head waiter recover and come hurrying to escort him to the door; but he didn't catch Rollison up.

Rollison reached the terrace.

It had been hot inside the dining-room, and the evening air was cool. The orchestra was having a rest. The big crowd in the street was waiting for the next playing session.

Rollison crossed the road. A *fiacre* passed, the lovers in it sitting very close together. An idyll. The sea murmured. The orchestra started to play. A little pudding of a woman in a dark suit followed Rollison across the road, and stood near him when he leaned against the rail, looking out to sea. Some people were bathing, laughter floated upwards.

"Hallo, Fifi," said the Toff. "How is Simon?"

"Simon is a fool," declared Fifi Leclair, but she spoke

without conviction. "And you are a bigger fool, M. Rollison. I have a message for you."

"Yes?"

"In the whisky, arsenic."

The orchestra's tune sounded louder here than it had inside the dining-room. It drowned most other sounds. But the words of Simon's wife seemed very loud, each syllable thrust itself into Rollison's mind.

"*In the whisky, arsenic.*"

"I'm not surprised," he said very quietly. "Fifi, do you know what I would do, if I were you?"

"Invite for myself more trouble!"

"No," said Rollison, and turned to look at her. She barely came up to his shoulder. She had a round, chubby face and pretty eyes and fluffy hair; once she had been a pretty young thing, now she was a matron—and a perfect foil for Simon's clowning. "No, Fifi. I'd go back to Paris. I'd tell the *Baccarat* that you can't stay on the Riviera. Say there is some trouble in your family, say anything you like. Go away from here. Because the pace is getting hotter, and I don't want my friends to get hurt."

"If I tell that to Simon, he will blow the raspberry," declared Fifi. "So." A rasping sound offended the night air, but her expression didn't change. "How can we help more, *m'sieu*?"

"Go back to Paris."

"How, *m'sieu*?"

"Find Violette somewhere else to stay, or move yourselves. Deny that you know me."

"How can we help, *m'sieu*?"

"Two people have been brutally murdered."

"What is it that we can *do*?" asked Fifi, still without a change of tone or expression.

Rollison found himself chuckling, partly with relief.

"Very well, you win! Ask Simon to find out all he can about the Comte de Vignolles, who owns the *Baccarat* and is

frightened of competition. That's why he's brought Simon
and you and other artistes down here—to kill that competition stone dead. Why is he afraid of it? Does he use the
Baccarat to lure pretty girls down here, and then spirit
them away to the North African coast? Is he being should-
ered out of that racket? Don't probe too dangerously, just
find out more about the *Baccarat*—that's reasonable enough,
as you're going to work there. Dig out the things that the
police wouldn't hear about. All clear?"

"Very well, we shall try," promised Fifi. "And you? Will
you stay at the San Roman, or will you go somewhere else,
where they do not know how to find you?" Now her tone
changed—she became pleading in turn. "Do not make more
trouble than you already have. Protect yourself."

"Soon enough," said Rollison, "but I'll stay at the San
Roman for a little while longer. Where's that whisky
bottle?"

"At the hotel desk, waiting for you."

"That's fine," said Rollison. "I think I'll send it to the
police, and have them analyse it for themselves, and ask for
protection. Do you think that would be a good idea?"

Her eyes were suddenly radiant.

"If only you would, *m'sieu*!" she cried.

*   *   *   *   *

Rollison left Fifi, and went back to the hotel. There was a
strange look in the eyes of the staff, as if they could not believe that such a gentleman as Rollison could have walked
out on M. le Comte. Even Alphonse was slightly cool when
he handed back the bottle, with an envelope fastened round
it by a rubber band; that would be the analyst's report.

It was past time the police were told a little; not too much.
Violette's name had to be kept from them.

He stood in the lift, with the corsetted lift-boy studiously
avoiding his eye. He watched the landings, but nothing
happened; the constant awareness of danger could become a

wearing thing. If he asked for police protection it would help a little; could even help a lot. The police would give him a kind of 'protection'. Chicot would have to be much more careful.

But the danger was here, everywhere, like men watching and ready to snipe at him.

He opened the door of his room an inch, paused, listened, and heard the faintest of faint sounds from inside.

Someone was in there, hiding in the darkness.

15

NEWS IN ADVANCE

ROLLISON did not waste a moment then. If he closed the door he would tell whoever it was that he had been warned. So he pushed the door wide, then knelt down swiftly. He held his breath. Nothing would have surprised him then: the slash of a knife, the flash of a gun, the hiss of an automatic air-pistol. None of these things happened.

He took out the lethal cigarette-lighter.

He knew exactly where the switch was, put a finger on it, pressed, and stepped swiftly into the bathroom.

Light flooded the room, someone gasped—and silence followed.

Rollison slammed the passage door with his foot.

"*Who—who is that?*" a man whispered.

He was French, for only a Frenchman could speak with that accent. There was nervousness in the tone, a quaver in the voice. Something suggested that he was young. Rollison, beginning to sweat now that the emergency seemed past, answered abruptly:

"Rollison. Who are you?"

There was a pause. Then:

"I am Gérard," the speaker said.

That might be true; it sounded so. Rollison moved to-wards the other side of the bathroom door, so that he could see the entrance to the bedroom.

"Come to the door, and hold your hands in front of you."

After a slow movement, Gérard appeared. His fair hair seemed unnaturally light, the 'nice lad' look was spoiled by his nervousness. He kept licking his lips. He held his hands in front of him, and they were unsteady—the hands of a frightened man. Why had he taken such a wild chance?

"All right, relax," said Rollison, and moved to the pass-age door, shot the bolt, and turned back to the main room. "Why did you come here?"

He stepped into the bedroom.

Then he saw the depth of his folly.

Two brown-skinned men, very like the two who had climbed aboard the *Maria*, were behind the door. One showed a knife, the other a wooden club. They watched him closely, warily.

Gérard leapt forward, as if he were terrified of what the Toff would do, and as he turned round he cried:

"I had to do it, they tortured me!"

"So you had to do it," said the Toff. Nothing in the world would ever sound more contemptuous. "May your con-science for ever——" He broke off. "Oh, what the hell! I ought to have expected it. What are the riff-raff here for?"

Words bubbled out of the Frenchman.

"You—you have to come with me. They're to make sure that you do. If you don't, they'll kill—they'll kill you!"

"And where are we supposed to go?"

"The Villa Seblec," Gérard said. His teeth chattered. "They made me tell them; I tried to hold out, but I couldn't."

Rollison didn't answer.

He looked at the two brown-skinned men, concentrating

on the one with the knife. His heart was hammering. The worst of the situation was that they were on different sides of the door, could attack from two directions. They had moved a little nearer; threateningly. He did not know whether to believe Gérard or not. They were more likely to follow him out of the hotel, let him start out for the Villa Seblec, and then—a knife in his back, his body tossed over the rocks and into the sea.

Neither of them spoke.

"Can they speak English?" Rollison asked, and slid his right hand towards his pocket; and the lighter.

"I speak English," one man said. "Take your hand away, quick," It was like 'queek'. "Go now, wis Gérard."

There was no certainty that Rollison would get out of the hotel alive, but obviously they would prefer to kill somewhere else, where the body could be hidden.

Yet they'd tried to poison him.

Why hadn't Gérard waited alone, lured him out, and spotlighted him for an attack?

One answer was obvious: that Chicot didn't trust Gérard. Was that all?

Rollison said: "I want a cigarette, and you can do what you damned well like." He took out his cigarette-case and the lethal lighter. The Arab who had spoken held the knife as if to throw it; but he didn't. The cigarette-case and lighter were in the Toff's hands. He began to sweat. He opened the cigarette-case, put a cigarette to his lips, and then made as if to light it. He moved, so that he could see both Arabs. The man with the knife was nearer. One of the tiny bullets in the eye would blind, one in his neck might kill. One in his hand——

Rollison flicked the lighter.

The *click*! was like an ordinary lighter-sound. There was just a wisp of flame. The tiny bullet struck the hand holding the knife, and as the Arab cried out, Rollison spun round. The other Arab was already moving, club raised. In that vivid moment, Rollison knew how the brown-eyed beggar had been killed.

He didn't fire, but jumped forward, crashed bodily into the man, and carried him back. The impact jolted the Arab, whose club fell. Rollison raised both hands and gripped the lean brown throat, then crashed the man's head against the wall. The thud was dull and sickening, and the dark eyes rolled. Rollison let the man slide down the wall, unconscious, and turned sharply. The other Arab, knife in his left hand, was moving towards him.

The lighter——

Gérard shot out a leg.

The Arab kicked against it, and fell sprawling. The Toff let him pass, then clipped him sharply behind the ear to help him on his way.

Gérard watched with rounded eyes and rounded mouth, as if he couldn't believe what he had done.

"Thanks," said Rollison, not even slightly out of breath; "there's hope for you yet." He moved quickly to the telephone. "Get out, wait for me in the toilets. I'm going to call the police."

"But——"

Rollison didn't look at him, but spoke into the telephone. The operator said: "At once, *m'sieu*," then came back on the line, puzzled. "The *Commissariat de Police*, *m'sieu*?"

"Please, and quickly," said Rollison.

The second Arab was picking himself up, but was a long way from his knife, which lay on the floor.

"Hurry, Gérard," said Rollison; "they'll soon be here. Tread on that knife before you go."

Gérard hesitated.

Then abruptly he moved forward, and stamped his heel on the shining blade. It broke. He stamped again and again in sudden fury, 'then went out, his face a flaming red.

One Arab was unconscious, the other watched the lighter in Rollison's hands as if he expected it to spit fire.

A man answered . . .

"*M. l'Inspecteur*, if you please," said Rollison. He knew that his name would be known, for he had worked in the South of France before. The police would listen to him, and the police would soon be here.

There was a pause, followed by a deeper voice. Rollison talked briskly. There were two Arab thieves whom he had surprised in his room, would *M. l'Inspecteur* . . .

M. l'Inspecteur most certainly would! What hotel?

Soon Rollison replaced the receiver. His expression hadn't changed. The expression of the Arab hadn't, either. It was not the man who could speak English; he was still unconscious by the wall. They stood watching each other. If the man made a dive for the door, it wouldn't be easy to stop him. These pellet-bullets were too scarce to be wasted, and would not stop a man unless they struck exactly the right place.

He should have used Gérard more.

Rollison moved slowly, seeing the club on the floor near the claw-like hand of the unconscious man. The other saw what he was going to do, then took a desperate chance and ran towards the door.

Rollison snatched up the club and threw it. The thick end caught the Arab on the back of the head. He pitched forward, shouting out more with fear than pain. Rollison went after him, picked him up by his collar and the seat of his trousers, and bustled him into the bathroom. Then he slammed and locked the door.

The other man was still unconscious.

A waiter came, in alarm . . .

.   .   .   .   .

All that Rollison could tell the police about le Comte de Vignolles was that they had dined and talked, and the Count had called himself M. Blanc. All he could say about Chicot was that a girl whose reputation wasn't exactly unsullied had said he was bad. He could tell of the murdered beggar, but the body would have been taken away by now. He could say that Suzanne had been murdered, and the police would be polite but incredulous, because she had fallen from the window.

The safest thing was to tell part of the truth; his suspicions of the 'accident' on the promenade, the attempt to poison him, and the visit of the two Arabs. The police would have to take him seriously.

He had never felt that he needed help more; for not one, but many girls had disappeared.

Were they alive?

Or were they dead?

.   .   .   .   .

Rollison had met Inspector Panneraude on a previous visit to Nice; a brisk, middle-aged man, as lean as Rollison himself, aware of the soubriquet 'Toff' and much that went with it. He took it all very seriously, and ventured to say that he had personally investigated the 'accident', and whatever one might suspect, no one could prove it had been intentional. Several witnesses had seen a little dog. . . .

The Inspector hoped M. Rollison had told all the truth. Why was he in Nice? The story of the missing girl satisfied him, or appeared to; the two Arabs were taken off, hand-cuffed, the other police went out. When they had all gone, the Inspector became much more a human being, and accepted a glass of the wine which Rollison had bought for Simon Leclair.

"*Merci bien, m'sieu!* Your very good health and safety in France!" He held up his glass and beamed; then drank. "Ah, this *very* good." He read the label on the bottle, nodded as with a connoisseur's approval, and changed the subject briskly. "These Arabs, we have very much trouble with them. Some have French passports, of course, although many of them cannot speak a word of French. Others come from

Spanish Morocco. They are brought here as servants because they will work almost for nothing; we have too many of them, far too many. We try to control their entry, but the Spanish are smuggled ashore at lonely spots, so what can we do? These two—were they just thieves, or was it connected with this whisky, do you think?"

It was a deliberately naïve question.

"I wouldn't know," said Rollison mildly. "I hope you'll find out."

"But of course, *m'sieu!*" The Inspector smiled wryly, as if he appreciated the *naïveté* of evasion. "Is there anything else I can do for you?"

"There's one thing," Rollison said. "Will you telephone M. Chicot at the Villa Seblec, explain who you are, and say that I have been delayed, but hope to get there later?"

"You are sure he lives there?"

"It'll be a way to find out."

"But you are free to go at once, *m'sieu.*"

"I'd like M. Chicot or others at the Villa to know that the delay wasn't my own fault," said Rollison. "I'd like them to know I'm with the police. It might be—ah—safer."

"But of course, I understand." The Inspector moved to the telephone. "Chicot," he echoed. "I remember there was a cabaret star named Chicot, some years ago; he was very funny. So droll. Only one man in all France was ever funnier than Chicot, and that is Simon Leclair. Leclair will be here next week—now there is a man to see! At the *Baccarat.*"

The operator answered; Panneraude asked for the Villa Seblec, and held on. "Yes, Simon Leclair will appear at the *Baccarat,*" he repeated. "That is owned by M. le Comte de Vignolles. Am I permitted an indiscretion? . . . 'Allo, M. Chicot, please. . . . He does not? Then M. Morency. . . . Dr. Morency, I am sorry. Be good enough to pass on this message. I am *Inspecteur* Panneraude of the *Commissariat de Police.* . . . Yes, *Inspecteur* Panneraude. . . . I speak for Mr. Richard Rollison, who has had a burglary at his hotel and is delayed. Please tell Dr. Morency. . . . You are sure M. Chicot does not live there?"

He rang off.

He had been eyeing Rollison very thoughtfully; shrewdly. As he put the receiver down, he went on:

"The maid who answered does not know a M. Chicot. You heard that. The other—is it permitted?"

"The indiscretion? Of course."

"Tonight you had the honour of dining with M. le Comte de Vignolles," said Panneraude musingly. "You left him abruptly, and it is said that you insulted him. Would you like to tell me why you quarrelled, M. Rollison?"

Rollison murmured: "He would like to find out who Chicot is, and offered a fat fee."

"Fee, *m'sieu*?"

"I thought it would be as well to find out if it were a bribe."

"So you did not like M. le Comte?"

"I don't yet know him well enough to be sure."

"What else did he say?"

"That girls who perform at the *Baccarat* go to the Villa Seblec, and don't come back."

"And," Panneraude said soberly, "that is true."

"Have you ever visited the Villa?"

"We have no evidence of crimes committed there," Panneraude countered smoothly.

"But suspicion?"

"We suspect so many people. Now, of the other gentleman. I confess that I would like to quarrel with M. le Comte myself. He has great wealth, he is of great influence, but I am not convinced that he is above suspicion. If it is possible to suggest any—shall we say any little misdemeanour on his part which would enable the police to make some investigation of his affairs, the *Département* would be very grateful to you."

Rollison was smiling.

"So you don't like him either."

"*M'sieu*, one is a policeman. One does not like any gentlemen who regard themselves as above the law. One lives perpetually in the hope that such gentlemen will make the important mistake which will enable the law to show interest. If such a thing should happen . . ." He broke off.

"If it should happen," promised Rollison, "you would be the first person I told."

"Thank you a thousand times, *m'sieu*. And now I must go." Panneraude moved towards the door. "This English girl, Daphné Myall. You understand, do you not, that she appeared for a little time at the *Baccarat*, which is owned by our friend M. le Comte? It was after that that she disappeared. The manager said that she was dismissed, as not good enough, and he knows no more of her. Have you found out more, *m'sieu*?"

"Not yet."

"I earnestly ask you to believe that the services of the police will be at your disposal if you should require them in the pursuit of justice, and I shall detail men to watch you," said Panneraude solemnly. "*Au revoir, m'sieu!*"

His handclasp was very firm.

.   .   .   .   .

There was nothing firm about Gérard Bourcy, when Rollison brought him from the magnificent splendour of the bathrooms. He was trembling, smoking, and licking his lips. Yet he had shot out a foot and perhaps saved Rollison from the business end of that Arab's knife. There was some good stuff in him.

"What happened in the cabin cruiser?" Rollison demanded.

"It—it was as you said," muttered Gérard. "One man came, and later, two more. The boat was taken back, we came round when we were back at the Villa."

"And then?"

"I tried to do what you ask, but I could not," said Gérard

tensely. "Understand, *m'sieu*, my own sister is in danger. There is much evil there; girls who come and—vanish! I am not strong enough. I am told to come to talk to you here, and —and you know what followed."

"Yes, I know. Well—I'm going to the Villa Seblec," Rollison announced and saw astonishment leap into Gérard's eyes. "I'll have police protection, which should help. You can go back and tell them what happened here, or you can stay here in hiding."

"What—what do you think I ought to do?" muttered Gérard; he found it difficult even to ask the question.

"Go back," said Rollison. "Telephone them first, say that the Arabs made a hash of the job but you escaped, and ask them for more orders. Don't tell them you know I'm on the way."

Gérard said miserably: "I am so afraid."

"Gérard," said Rollison gently, "your sister is in danger. So are you. So are these other girls. You have a chance to help them all and wipe the slate clean. With you at the Villa, to help in a crisis, the impossible might become possible."

"I—I will try," Gérard promised, and tried to square his shoulders.

Rollison said: "You'll do it, Gérard. One thing before you go. Is the Comte de Vignolles known at the Villa?"

"Known?" echoed Gérard. "He is hated!"

"Do you know why?"

"No," Gérard answered, "to me the Villa is full of mystery and evil things."

"We'll clean it up," said Rollison, but he had to force the note of confidence in his voice. He went towards the door. Gérard started to speak, but didn't; Rollison went out.

A *gendarme*, big revolver in his shiny holster, stood just outside, saluting.

"Where do we go, *m'sieu*?"

"The Villa Seblec," said Rollison, as brightly. "If I go in my car, will you follow in a taxi?"

"Whichever you wish, *m'sieu*," said the policeman, and he walked step by step with Rollison to the lift. "There will be two of us, all the time."

16

THE VILLA SEBLEC

THE moon was up, and bathed the Ile de Seblec with a soft light which quickened the pulse of all but cynics. The garden had been beautiful that afternoon; it was lovely now, although the colours no longer flamed. The Villa itself was gently floodlit, and stood out clearly at the tip of the Ile as Rollison, driving a hired Jaguar, drove along the main road. The Villa fell out of sight just about the spot where he had climbed the wall—and left a taxi-driver, who would have given him up a long time ago.

They turned on to the private road.

The other car, with the policeman in it, was only fifty yards behind. It had stopped, to let one policeman get out at a spot where he could watch the house. There had been very little traffic, nothing at all to hint at trouble.

The headlights of Rollison's car fell upon the back of the Villa Seblec. No one was in sight. The back door was closed. A path led to the front door, the one which had opened when Violette had run away from here, and Rollison followed this, looking about the grounds and towards the spot where the beggar had lain.

He rang the bell.

After a pause, a maid answered ; she was a middle-aged woman in black, with a tiny white apron and lace cap. Obviously she expected him.

"M. Sautot is not at home," she said, "but Dr. Morency is. Will you see him?"

"Please," said Rollison gravely.

"This way, *m'sieu*."

"Thank you. Will you be good enough to allow my escort to wait outside?" added Rollison. "He is from the *Commissariat de Police*." He beamed. "If he could have a glass of good red wine, he would be grateful."

"It shall be done, *m'sieu*."

"You are very good."

The Toff stepped into the hall.

The first glance told him that this was not just another villa; this was the home of a millionaire, and had probably been built at a time when money had not mattered. One did not have to like the Bacchanalian *motif* in order to admire the magnificence of the painting—dark brown upon cream walls —or the carved recesses, from whence the light came; or in the ceiling itself. It reminded him vaguely of the villas at Pompeii; there was much beauty, much loveliness of design, of sculpture and painting; but everything was slightly tainted; corrupted.

Was that because of what he knew about Dr. Morency, about Raoul, and about some of the things that were believed to happen here?

The lights were concealed inside nude figures; or some part of the human form, and carved out of alabaster or made of lovely handblown glass—some green, some pale amber. There were no pictures, just the recesses—and the carvings inside them showed all that was beautiful in the art of France and much that corrupts in the worship of art.

In its way, this was like the ante-room of a palace.

A man came, briskly. Rollison did not believe that the old doctor could walk with such speed.

It was not Morency, but Raoul.

In some ways, Raoul was twice the man Gérard was, and he had recovered fully. His look was aggressive, there was an open sneer on his face. He was dressed in a well-cut suit of cream linen, and hadn't a black hair out of place.

"Hallo," greeted Rollison pleasantly. "Feeling better?"

"I am not feeling so well as I shall one day," said Raoul. "What do you want?"

"Chicot, or else——"

"No one named Chicot lives here."

"Poor clown," said Rollison. "Have you murdered him too? Who killed poor Gaston, Raoul? Was it the man who was to crack my head in like a piece of china?"

"Your head will crack soon enough." Raoul was roughly truculent. "And all the police in the *Commissariat* won't save you when we're ready! You'd better come this way." He turned and led the way out of the room, along a narrow passage which was decorated in exactly the same fashion, into a long, narrow room.

Rollison stopped, missing a step, for suddenly this room changed colour.

Raoul gave a savage grin.

"The hell *motif*," he sneered. "You'd better get used to it; you'll be visiting the real place soon enough."

Rollison hardly heard the words.

The lighting came from red glass or red porcelain, set in the floor, the ceiling, and the walls. Everything was washed in the same deep, blood red. Here the figures were different: Machiavellian, instead of Bacchanalian. Here were tiny statues of devils with cloven hoofs, worked into all the carving; all the paintings were the same, and lit with intense white light sharp against the general crimson. Carpet, polished floor, dadoed ceiling, and imitation windows, were all red. At the windows, fire seemed to blaze. It wasn't truly fire, but a simulation, and the light kept moving, flickering over the faces of the devils and the devils' angels.

Into this room shuffled Dr. Morency.

.   .   .   .   .

"I am glad to have the pleasure of meeting you, Mr. Rollison," said Dr. Morency. He had a gentle, lisping voice, gentle, tired eyes, tinged with red, and a soft-looking hand. Everything would have been gentle about him, had it not been for his face. Just as the devil was depicted in all the statues and the statuettes here, as well as in the paintings, so it was in Dr. Morency. If a man had said: "Meet Dr. Mephistopheles," no one would have been surprised.

He did not offer to shake hands.

"I wanted to see you, although I understand that you are under a misapprehension," went on Dr. Morency. "No one named Chicot lives here."

"That's hard," said Rollison. "I'd been told that I would find him." He took his cigarette-case out, and selected a cigarette with finicky care. He knew that, in spite of his truculence, Raoul was on edge; and Dr. Morency could hardly wait to hear what the visitor really wanted.

He asked: "Did you find my clothes by the beach, doctor?"

"Some clothes were found——"

"And the gun, I hope," Rollison murmured. "I was fond of that gun, but I can manage without it." He paused to let that sink in deeply. Then: "We've had quite a time, haven't we? Violette ran away from the clutching hands, your killers killed at sea, and others taken prisoner at the San Roman. I wonder what story they'll tell the police?" He laughed, and startled them; they watched him warily now, as if worried about what he would do next. "I had to come to France to ask for police protection, but it's there, remember; Panneraude knows. One policeman's outside, another is watching from the main road. The one thing you dare not do is to stop me from leaving. Agreed, doctor?"

"We have no desire——" began Dr. Morency smoothly.

"Doctor," said Rollison. Suddenly he looked and sounded savage, and he clutched at Morency's thin shoulder. "You are a liar. You are a degenerate. And you are a fool. Chicot's here, and I want Chicot. I also want Daphne Myall."

He pushed Morency back, and swung round on Raoul, the last thing the youth had expected. He snatched Raoul's arm and twisted, until Raoul clenched his teeth and began to bend at the knees. Then Rollison dipped into his pocket, touched an automatic pistol, and drew it out. He let Raoul go, and broke the chamber of the gun, making sure that it was loaded. He clicked it back into position, and beamed.

"Just what I wanted," he said. "Thanks. Doctor, I am now going to have a look through the Villa. I'm sure you won't mind. I could call the police to help me, of course, but there might be some little formalities if I do that. Shall I manage on my own?"

Raoul said thinly: "I'll kill you first!"

"But I have to leave here alive," murmured the Toff. "You see what a delicate situation it is. I have been attacked in my hotel. Attempts have been made to poison me. If there's trouble, I simply tell the police that I discovered you were responsible for the crimes. If I die, the police will have a long statement, delivered by a bank. It will tell everything I know about Chicot, Sautot, and you two, as well as a great many other little things. Will you come with me, doctor, or shall I go alone?"

He wasn't sure that they would let him go.

They were afraid of what he might find, and afraid of the police getting a reason for coming and searching. The whole of his gamble depended on which they feared most.

Morency said in his lisping voice.

"You must do what you think best, Mr. Rollison, but it is a big mistake to think that there is anything here to shame us." His hooded eyes blinked, and he rubbed his long, thin hands together. "And there is no other man here except us and one servant." He paused, moistened his lips, kept rubbing his hands, and then asked thinly: "Tell me what it is you wish to find; I may be able to help you."

E

"First, find me Chicot. . . . Then the English girl," said Rollison. "The girl named Myall."

Morency blinked.

"There is no one here named Chicot," he insisted, "no one at all. As for the girl Daphne——" He shrugged his narrow shoulders and wrung his Heep-like hands. Then he turned towards the door and muttered what sounded like an imprecation.

It opened, and Daphne Myall came in.

17

LITTLE GIRL LOST

THE thing that surprised Rollison, when the first shock was over, was her size. She was so tiny. She didn't lack anything in the way of a figure, for she was beautifully formed. In the flesh, she was lovelier than her photograph had suggested. She wore a strapless dinner-gown, leaving little to the imagination, yet it was not greatly different from many that might be seen in Mayfair.

Her fair hair was beautiful. If she poked her fingers through it a little more, it would be unruly; now, it was just right. It was really more golden than blond, and that showed even in the red lighting.

The lighting changed, to normal.

Daphne Myall looked at Rollison coldly. She had a tired look about her, the look of one who had just been woken out of a deep sleep; or perhaps, one who had been in a dark room or a cinema.

"Daphne, my dear," said Dr. Morency, "I would like you to meet Mr. Richard Rollison."

She hardly looked at Rollison. "Did you have to bring me out here?"

"Yes, I had to," said Morency. "Mr. Rollison would like you to leave the house with him. He would like to take you back home."

The sleepy look vanished, her eyes sparked, her tone was sharp; angry.

"Who the devil does he think he is?"

"As a matter of fact, my dear," said Morency, "he has a very high opinion of himself, and I would like you to help to deflate him."

Morency smiled; and so turned himself into a satyr.

"What is all this about?" the girl asked Rollison abruptly.

She was annoyed, she'd been discourteous, apparently she was puzzled. Yet there was something about her Rollison liked. Her voice was slightly husky, the product of a good school. She carried herself well. When one recovered from the shock of finding that she was so tiny, she was likely to grow on one.

"I had a job to do, for your mother and father," Rollison said.

"Oh, *no*!"

"Didn't you expect them to be worried about you?"

She looked at him steadily. She had big eyes shaded with mascara, and very blue; he remembered Myall's being as blue.

"No," she said, deliberately, "I didn't expect them to care a damn about me. I don't think they do."

"You're wrong, you know. Your mother——"

"I'm sorry," Daphne Myall said firmly, "I don't want to hear any more about them. I made the break, and it is final. I don't think they were surprised; certainly my mother wasn't. I'm sorry if you've wasted your time, but there it is. Will you excuse me?"

She turned on her heel and went out. The door closed softly behind her.

The lights changed again, to a pale blue, and succeeded in making Dr. Morency look a most unhealthy creature, and in making Raoul look ill. He was grinning with that restrained savagery which characterised him.

"Satisfied?" he sneered. "There's your missing girl. That's how grateful she is to you for putting your nose into her business."

"I noticed it," murmured Rollison. "Little Girl Lost and she doesn't know it."

In fact, he was on very dangerous, shifting ground. He had expected all kinds of things, but hadn't dreamed of this. Daphne seemed to be as free as she could be; a willing 'prisoner'. She wasn't the first girl to have left home because she had quarrelled with her mother or felt stifled by the home atmosphere, and she wouldn't be the last. There was nothing to indicate that anything she had said had been under duress. Neither Rollison nor the police could make her leave.

"Now you can tell her parents that she is safe and well," murmured Dr. Morency. "I am sure that in the circumstances there is nothing else you require here."

"I can't wait to show you out," Raoul said.

Rollison beamed at them.

"Oh, not yet; I want to look round. If you keep this up, I may be able to give you a reference as a home for Nice Young Ladies."

The thing that worried him, and was likely to for a long time, was the way the ground had shifted from under him. If he'd seen Daphne Myall twenty-four hours before, he would have gone back to England and reported that there was nothing he could do. She'd been kept out of the way until then.

Now——

He began to smile.

They had cause for alarm; greater cause, now that he had called upon the police. They were frightened of what might

happen if he and the police probed too far. He had come for
Daphne Myall, and they had produced her, hoping that it
would satisfy him, that he would have no further cause to
probe.

Only desperate men would have done that. Probably their
position was weaker than he had realised.

"There is nothing here that will interest you," said Dr.
Morency flatly.

"My interests are flung so far and wide," said Rollison
brightly, "you'd be surprised how many things they include." He raised his eyebrows, for the lighting changed
again, becoming red. "Don't you find this spotlighting a
little trying?" He lit another cigarette. "Forgive the
banality, but would you mind showing me where your cloak-
room is? Ah—toilet."

"Raoul, show Mr. Rollison," said Dr. Morency. The lisping voice wasn't at all satyrish, nor was his tired manner.
But it had to be remembered that Violette thought him more
evil than Raoul. This old man!

Morency stood in the middle of the red-tinged room,
washing his hands softly, as Raoul led Rollison along a narrow
passage, round a corner, to a closed door. With exaggerated
courtesy, Raoul opened the door. The toilet was large, faced
with green tiles with a handbasin and towels, and with a
ventilation grille, but no window.

"Exactly right," said Rollison. "After you."

Rollison let his hand fall on to the Frenchman's wrist, and
twisted; Raoul found himself propelled into the closet. It
was easy because it was the last thing Raoul expected. He
was still staggering when Rollison took the key out of the
inside of the lock, closed the door, and locked it. He was
at the door of the red-lit room when the first shout came,
but the door, tightly sealed, kept it down to a subdued
murmur.

Dr. Morency was just standing.

"Hallo, Doc," said Rollison, and made the old man swing

round. "Raoul's having a rest; I thought it would be nice to be alone. Do you mind taking me to the room where Daphne is?"

Morency gaped.

"Unless you'd rather I put you to sleep and foraged round for myself," suggested Rollison. "That would take longer." He took out the automatic which he had taken from Raoul, and put it back. "It would blow a big hole through you—like the hole in Sautot's hand. Where is poor Sautot, by the way?"

"He—he is away," Morency choked. "His hand is so bad —Rollison, what do you want?"

"Chicot."

"There is no one here named Chicot!"

"I'll make sure for myself," said Rollison, and took the old man's arm. It seemed to be all bone and gristle. "What about his friend, the Comte de Vignolles?"

Morency winced:

"*That* criminal? That——" He didn't finish.

"Could thieves have fallen out, I wonder," murmured the Toff. "But let's get a move on, I don't mind where we start."

As in a dream, Morency led the way . . .

.   .   .   .   .

Fabulous was the word.

Each room had a different *motif*; each room had beauty of colour and line, and each that faintly corrupted atmosphere; it was impossible to say exactly why. The dining-room was long and narrow with a table which could seat a dozen on either side and one at each end and, unexpectedly, was in Louis Quinze style. The huge murals were of French Court scenes; not the most licentious kind, but quite licentious enough. Library, morning-rooms on the ground floor, *salons* and bedrooms on the floor above, were all very much the same. Comfort, luxury, beauty. Even the kitchens were modern to the last word, with chromium and coloured tiles. A staff of four, all women, were on duty there.

But Morency had not taken him to see Daphne Myall.

Morency talked . . .

"I do not know why you have become so hostile, Mr. Rollison. I assure you that there is no need for it. We are not criminals. You saw Violette running away from here, but Violette——" He touched his forehead. "It was necessary to try to stop her from leaving. You understand? And of course we tried to get her back. Whoever is with her now will find out that she isn't quite sane; she will appear sane for a few hours or perhaps a few days, and then——" He shrugged. "The truth will become apparent."

"So you're just good, honest citizens," said Rollison.

"In our way, Mr. Rollison, yes. You talk of violence—*we* are not responsible. Of attempts to poison you—*we* did not make them. Of Arabs who come to attack you—*we* employ no Arabs. It is all a big mistake."

They were back in the Room of Devils. The lighting was white now; it had been for some time, the automatic switching system obviously wasn't working. Morency just looked a tired old man, with wrinkled skin and a raddled face, more disappointed lecher now than satyr.

"Where is Daphne?" asked Rollison sharply.

"Oh, she must have gone out; she may be swimming," said Morency, spurred to a touch of impatience. "She is not kept here against her will."

That was almost convincing.

He was standing in the same spot that he had when Rollison had first come in. He kept there, most of the time, in the middle of the room. He was near a chair, and occasionally he sat on the arm. Something about the way he seemed to be locked to the spot made Rollison look about him carefully.

"Come and see for yourself," Dr. Morency invited.

He led the way to the wide loggia which overlooked the

garden and, some distance off, the sea. The moon spread its softening light—and even softened the *gendarme* who sat on a stone seat, with a large bottle and a glass by his side; he appeared to be communing with the stars. As the two men appeared, he jumped up.

"*Messieurs!*"

"Has a young lady come out here?" asked Rollison.

"But yes, *m'sieu!*" One could tell from the tone of this man's voice that the young lady was really *some*thing. Dr. Morency let his hands slide together. *Sss-sss-sss*. Rollison strolled towards the end of the garden. Nearing the jetty, he heard a splash. He reminded himself that this was the path along which Violette had run, chased by Sautot, who had tried to shoot her and so prevent her from escaping.

He knew that everything Morency had said was a lie, but it wasn't going to be easy to prove.

For there was Daphne Myall.

She was climbing up wooden steps to the jetty, and didn't look at him. The moonlight glistened on her wet body. She wore a pink bathing-cap and a pink *bikini*—so natural in colour that at first she appeared to be stark naked. She went to the side of the jetty, poised on the edge, and dived in.

She made little sound.

"She is happy here," declared Dr. Morency. "Everyone is happy here. Why do you persecute us, Mr. Rollison?" *Sss-sss-sss*.

"Why did you kill the beggar, and why did you try to kill Violette?"

"I have said all that I can say," declared Dr. Morency, "and shown you everything there is to show. I am sorry, there is nothing else that I can do."

He turned and walked away. He didn't hurry. His hands swung loosely by his sides, and his narrow shoulders were hunched. His footsteps hardly sounded. The ripple of water as the girl whom Rollison had come to find swam back to the steps was the loudest sound. Not far off, the moon shimmered on the gently moving sea.

The girl climbed up again.

Morency had left him here to talk to her alone, as if he wanted to make it clear, without another word, that she was free to talk, to do exactly what she liked.

Rollison waited at the top of the steps. She climbed up, moving superbly. That inbred courtesy prevented her from pushing past him, as she obviously wanted to.

"Miss Myall," Rollison said, "I would like to take a message back to your parents. What shall it be?"

She said slowly:

"You can tell them that I am happier here than I have ever been. Much, much happier."

Then she pointed downwards to the post at the top of the steps. He didn't guess why, but realised that there was a difference about her; a great tension. She moved to pass him, went close to the edge, and slipped.

"Steady!" he cried.

She grabbed his arm, to save herself, and he leaned back to take the strain. Out of the pulsing silence she whispered two words. He felt the warmth of the breath in his ear, and doubted whether he had heard aright.

"*Fall in*," she whispered. "*Fall in*."

She toppled backwards, let go of his arm, and dropped. Water splashed up, drenching him.

He had to go in after her, or stand and watch. The second in which the decision had to be made dragged out for an age.

The gun would get wet, and the lighter. He——

He was swaying towards the water, as if off his balance, pretended to slip and went down feet first. As the water closed about him, he felt the clutch of fear.

If he drowned, Panneraude would never believe, but might have to accept the verdict: "*Accident*."

18

WHISPER ON THE WATER

HE felt no hand against him, no hand dragging at him, no pressure, no sense of danger beyond the one that was in his own mind. He surfaced and trod water. His clothes were sodden, and he couldn't swim for long. He could just see Daphne Myall striking out towards him; there was no one else. The water was warm, and yet he shivered; for in this translucent light he would not be able to see a swimming Arab even if one was near.

The girl drew close.

"Sorry I—tripped you," she said, and her voice was unexpectedly loud. "Stubbed my—toe." She sounded breathless, but she wasn't, for next moment she was holding on to him and her lips were close to his ear. "*Ten others are here. Get us away,*" she breathed. Then without a pause and much more loudly: "The steps are over here. Hurry."

The steps were in sight.

"I'm all right," Rollison said; "don't worry about me." Then in a whisper: "*Where?*"

"What a crazy thing to do!" she exclaimed, as if really angry with herself. "*Inside the cliff.* Don't bump your head. *If the police come, we'll all be killed.*"

That was—crazy. Wasn't it?

Rollison bumped his shoulder against the rail of the steps, turned, clutched it, and pulled himself up. Close to the foot of the post, he saw a cable—as for electricity. Near that, let into the post, a small, gauze-covered hole.

That told him one secret; it was a microphone. The jetty and the garden, probably the rooms as well, were wired; and anything said out here would be carried to the Villa.

No wonder she had whispered!

Rollison heard footsteps clattering on the boards, then the heavy breathing of a man. It was the policeman, rushing up.

"*M'sieu Rollison, are you there?*"

Rollison's head appeared above the level of the jetty. The big man came hurrying, and knelt down to help him up. Rollison talked, fast. He was a fool, he'd slipped in trying to save Miss Myall from falling; as if it would have mattered! Brrh; it was colder than he thought. He needed fresh clothes. *Brrh!* But he turned and looked at Daphne Myall as she came to the jetty, and his voice hardened.

"As for you, you deserve all you get," he said. "I'll be at the San Roman until tomorrow, if you decide to change your mind." He shivered again. "I must get warm."

At the Villa, Morency was sauve and helpful; there was a spare suit of a man who sometimes stayed here; Mr. Rollison was welcome to borrow it. And a word in Mr. Rollison's ear: beware of Raoul. He did not find it possible to blame the youth, who obviously felt viciously angry because of the way he had been treated.

Beware of Raoul . . .

.   .   .   .   .

Rollison sat in the police car, the borrowed clothes too large for him. He smoked and welcomed the cool air off the sea. The two policemen were behind him, one of them in a new kind of seventh heaven because he was allowed to drive the Jaguar.

Had Daphne told the truth? Could she have any purpose in lying?

If microphones were about the garden, in the house, and even on the jetty, picking up all that was said and carrying it back into the Villa, she would need to whisper. She had looked well, and seemed to be telling the truth when they had first met, but—that tune had changed.

"*Ten others are here; get us away.*"

If he brought the police, and Daphne talked to them as

she had to him, the Villa wouldn't be searched. If it were, could the police find anything that he had missed?

"Where are they?"

"Inside the cliff."

"If the police come, they'll all be killed."

She hadn't sounded or acted as if she were mad. She had worked cunningly for the chance to whisper, and so defeat the ever-open ears. It was easier to believe than to disbelieve her.

He didn't know enough.

It had been eerie when it had happened, but was much worse now. He had left her behind, with her fears. His own were greater, for if she had told the truth, there were ten girls or more in acute danger.

The headlights of the car, yellow and dim, did not throw very far, but they lit up the hillside of the corniche road. Now and again they disappeared as they fell upon the parapet which protected the road from a steep fall on to rocks or into the sea.

Yes, it was much more eerie now.

.   .   .   .   .

"And you searched the house but found nothing, only saw this Miss Myall?" said Panneraude. He was in Rollison's room, tunic collar loosened, leather belt undone, revolver resting against the back of his chair. In his hand was a glass of that perfect wine. His helmet was off, and his hair proved to be iron grey. In his middle-aged way, he was quite handsome. "Mr. Rollison, may I tell you one or two things?"

"All you can," said Rollison. "Please. I feel as if I'm the most ignorant man in the world."

"You are disappointed because you found a way into the Villa Seblec, and thought that it would help you to find a way of putting an end to such an affair as this," said Panneraude. "I know the feeling. Once"—he sat up, spread his

fingers wide, and placed them against his chest—"*I* found a
reason for visiting the Villa Seblec. I took six men. What did
I find? Nothing? No, *m'sieu*, I found much, much worse
than nothing. I found that they laughed at me. They had
been warned and were prepared. What goes on there? I do
not know, but I am a policeman, and a policeman has a nose
to smell badness." He shifted his hands and nipped his
nose. "*Ugh!*"

Rollison didn't speak.

"Now you come, you try, you are disappointed." Panneraude shrugged. "'This year, next year, perhaps the people
there, like M. le Comte de Vignolles and his friends, will
make the important mistake. You will be in London, I,
Panneraude will be here! Tell me, did you guess anything
more than you have told me?"

He couldn't tell Panneraude yet.

"No."

"Always the same," said Panneraude, sipping his wine
again. "Beautiful young women who disappear. I tell you
another thing. The daughter of an important Army general
disappeared the other day. She was seen in Nice. She was
later seen on board a boat, called the *Nuit Verte*. To you,
the *Green Night*! We search, but do not find her. Tonight
the *Nuit Verte* returns to Cannes. It is boarded before
anyone disembarks, and is searched. No girl is found. No one
admits that she was ever on board. It was all a mistake!" He
shrugged. "That is how it always happens, M. Rollison."

"And you know nothing, beyond that?"

"One big thing," Panneraude said quietly. "Many of
these very beautiful girls disappear. Some, not so beautiful.
Nearly all are from high-born families, and bear great
names. They meet wealthy men, and, using their names to
win trust, they cheat these men. Most victims say nothing,
but some report to us. No one is anxious for scandal.
The girls sometimes return, as often are never heard of
again."

"How long has this been going on?" asked Rollison, and gave no hint that he had known anything about this; but inwardly he felt like purring, for Violette had not lied.

"For two years or more," Panneraude said. "That is the big thing I now have permission to tell you. There is also one *little* thing."

"What's that?" asked Rollison.

Panneraude seemed to expand.

"A certain Englishman comes to look for a certain English girl. When he arrives, Scotland Yard telephones to the police in Nice, to say that this man may appear to do foolhardy things, perhaps unlawful things, but that he will really try to help. They do not ask us to wink at anything he does; they just tell us that perhaps he will not be as black as he paints himself." Panneraude appeared to be wholly serious. "This Englishman is here for a few days. Then: *First*, he is nearly killed by a car driven by one Raoul Cyurol, who lives at the Villa Seblec. *Second*, he pays a very poor man, a beggar, to look for the English girl, and the beggar's body is found in the sea, a very ugly sight. Murder. *Third*, he is seen at sea aboard the *Maria* which belongs to the owner of the Villa Seblec, with a very beautiful young lady who is suspected, we cannot say more, of having swindled a wealthy Parisian last year. She sold him worthless shares, you understand—how do you say?"

"Bucket shop."

"Some other words."

"Confidence tricks."

"That is it—the tricks confidential. The man will not prosecute because, we believe, this young lady is the daughter of a great friend, but——" Panneraude shrugged. "*Fourth*, the Englishman dines with M. le Comte de Vignolles, and walks out on him. Fifth"—for a moment Panneraude was almost as droll-looking as Simon Leclair—"it is in the future. We send a telegram to Scotland Yard. 'Much regret well-meaning English private detective dead, advise us what to do with the body'."

He stopped.

Rollison was smiling appreciatively.

"Why do you not tell us everything?" Panneraude demanded explosively. "What do you fear? Don't you trust us?"

"My good friend Panneraude," said Rollison earnestly, "the very moment that I learn anything on which you can take action, I'll tell you. It isn't yet. If you should ever pull my body out of the deep blue sea, go and see Simon Leclair, the greatest clown of them all. He may know a little that you don't—about me," added Rollison hastily. "Only about me."

Panneraude went very still.

Rollison didn't like the look in his eyes. He didn't like the way he shrugged. He didn't like his attitude when he finished the wine which had been brought especially for the tall clown, and set the glass down.

"Do you trust Simon Leclair?" Panneraude asked.

"Of course I trust Simon Leclair."

"Good," said Panneraude, and stood up smartly. He fastened his tunic collar, and pulled the tunic down, then fastened his belt. "*Very* good. Perhaps you will ask him why he talked to Morency of the Villa Seblec this afternoon. Why he came twice into this room today, in your absence. Why he was here just before the poor child, Suzanne, fell to her death. And why he has arsenic in his room, in *le Pension Guy*," breathed the Frenchman. He took up an attitude which suggested he was quite prepared for Rollison to want to knock him down.

.   .   .   .   .

"Is all this certain?" asked Rollison heavily.

"Positive, *m'sieu*."

"The arsenic?"

"We are trying to find out where he bought it, *m'sieu*."

"Is he still at his *pension*?"

"We have reason to suspect him of some crime, but have not all the evidence," said Panneraude. "Also, we hope that he will lead us to the mistake which others will make. So, he is still at his *pension*."

"I think I'll go and see him," Rollison said.

"See him as often as you like," approved Panneraude, "but do not trust him one half-inch, M. Rollison." He held out his hand. "I am sorry. I know you have been friends with Simon Leclair for many years. It began, I understand, when his wife Fifi was accused of a betrayal of her employer, letting in the thieves who stole many millions of francs' worth of jewels. Thanks to you, Fifi proved her innocence." He shrugged. "Perhaps that also was a mistake, *m'sieu*. Perhaps you allowed your liking for the couple to influence your judgment. That is a luxury which the police cannot afford. *Au 'voir, m'sieu*."

.   .   .   .   .

It was nearly midnight.

A few people were left on the hotel terrace, drinking. The orchestra had gone, the crowd had gone, the staff looked tired. Rollison walked out of the main entrance. Fewer people than usual went out of their way to salute him; an affront to *M. le Comte* was, clearly, an affront to many others. He took the Jaguar, and drove into the heart of Nice behind the sea-front, to a spot near the big market. He left the car there, then waited for the police car which was following him.

Two different men were now on duty.

He walked briskly down a narrow street, where a single tram-track ran, looking at the ill-lit street signs. The fifth read: *Rue de Guy de Maupassant*. He turned down here. A few lighted signs read: *Auberge* or *Hotel* or *Pension*. One of the brightest of these was *le Pension Guy*. The front door was open. Just inside, sitting with a newspaper open on his lap, was a plump old *concierge*, wearing steel-rimmed glasses, a cotton jersey, blue jeans and plimsols cut so that his bunions could have full freedom.

He started to get up.

"Stay where you are," said Rollison, and smiled amiably. "I look for M. Simon Leclair."

"Oh, yes, *m'sieu*. The first floor, if you please; the second door on the right."

"Thank you."

"My pleasure, *m'sieu*."

The house smelt clean, the paint-work was fresh, everything suggested that it was as good as Simon Leclair had said. Rollison had not thought a great deal beyond what Panneraude had told him; there were some things which had to be assimilated slowly. This was one. He had not telephoned to say that he was coming, and Simon and Fifi might be in bed. He had not planned what he was going to say, either; he was going to try to form an opinion, to try to put Panneraude's accusations into clear perspective. Things that Simon might say could help.

Rollison tapped at the door.

There was no answer.

He tapped again, more loudly, and there was still no answer. He knew that the *concierge* would probably be tiptoeing to the foot of the stairs, to find out what he was doing, and that one of the policemen might be downstairs by now. So he hadn't long to work in. He took out a penknife, opened a blade which was in fact a skeleton key, flicked it into the lock, fiddled, and twisted. It was an old-fashioned lock, and opened within a few seconds.

He turned the handle of the door, hesitated, and then pushed it gently.

The room was in darkness.

He listened intently, and heard nothing. He felt sure that he would have detected it if anyone were breathing inside this first room. He went in, closed the door, and took out a small pencil torch. He shone the beam round. It shone upon armchairs, a carpet, a table. He found the electric light switch and pressed it down, and went in further.

Lying on a couch by the curtained window was Gérard Bourcy.

He was most obviously dead.

19

A CORPSE FOR A CLOWN

GÉRARD had been strangled. There were the dark bruises on his neck, to show it. His eyes were slightly open and glazed, and his mouth was slack. One hand drooped, the fingers touching the floor. His fair hair was untidy, and his knees were bent. His flesh wasn't yet cold.

Nothing moved; there was no sound.

Rollison turned round, reached the door again, paused, and then opened it. The *gendarme* was outside.

"*Pardon, m'sieu.*"

"I shall be here for some time. Don't let M. Leclair see you when he comes back."

"Very good, *m'sieu.*"

"Thank you," said Rollison.

He closed the door. He didn't greatly care what Panneraude thought or what the police thought; he wanted above everything else to be here when Simon returned, and to hear his comment.

If Simon had killed——

It wasn't possible to shut the thought out.

He moved from this room into the next, a large bedroom.

There was no kitchen and no bathroom, but another door led off the bedroom, which had a large single bed and would have been up to date in the middle of Queen Victoria's reign. Everything was Victorian, heavy, dark, typically pro-vincial French.

He tried the handle of the communicating door. It turned and the door wasn't locked. He opened it, cautiously. The dim light from this room fell on to a big wardrobe, a chair, and some oddments of woman's clothing. There was a whisper of even breathing.

He stepped inside.

Violette lay on the single bed in here, fast asleep, her hair looking strange because it had been bleached; there was no shadow of doubt that it was Violette.

Did she know that she was sleeping next to dead Gérard. Should he tell her ?

He went nearer the bed. There was a lamp at a bedside table, with a thick red silk shade. He switched it on. The light reminded him of the red lighting in the narrow room at the Villa Seblec. The way it fell upon Violette made her look younger. No, she wasn't a beauty, in the accepted sense; she just had—something.

He put a hand on her forehead.

"Violette," he said softly.

She didn't stir.

He moved his hand, touched her shoulder, and squeezed gently, ready to thrust his hand over her mouth if she should cry out.

She was heavily asleep.

He shook her more vigorously, and called more loudly: "*Violette!*"

She didn't take the slightest notice. He drew back, breath hissing, then went forward again, putting a thumb to her right eye, and raising the lid enough to be able to see the pupil. It was very small, as it might be if she had been drugged with morphia or a kindred drug.

Gérard dead and Violette drugged, and Simon and Fifi missing.

. . . . .

They did not return that night.

Rollison dozed much of it, in an easy-chair, with upright chairs at the doors, to make sure that he would be disturbed if anyone came in. No one did.

Violette woke just after seven o'clock.

. . . . .

She looked on Gérard's body, without saying a word. Rollison watched, and felt quite sure that she was utterly surprised. And it hurt her. She put her hands to her eyes and turned away blindly, took a step, then snatched her hands down fiercely, as if ashamed of the weakness.

"He was a coward and he is dead; who should worry?"

"Was he here when you went to bed?"

"No."

"Was Simon Leclair?"

"But of course, Simon and Fifi."

"What time did you go to bed?"

"It was early, I was very tired. Ten o'clock, when I came back from the hotel."

"Did you take a sleeping draught?"

"Fifi gave me some pills."

Fifi, Rollison remembered, had always slept badly, and always had a supply of sleeping pills.

"Did you talk about M. le Comte de Vignolles?"

"A little—nothing of importance. Why?" She stirred herself from a kind of mental numbness. "Why do you ask all these questions?"

"Better I than the police."

"The police! Are they——"

"They're outside," Rollison said, "but they don't know about this yet; we've a little time. You're quite sure that de Vignolles isn't a friend of Chicot?"

"Of course I am sure," she said. "Chicot has often talked of his dislike."

"All right," Rollison said. "I want you to get out of here. Leave a minute after me, and follow me to the covered market. Do you know it well?"

"I have been there."

"Are the flower-sellers all in one spot?"

"Yes."

"Meet me there," ordered Rollison. "Ignore the police if any are outside. Don't show any interest in me, but don't let me get out of your sight until we're at the market. Understand?"

"Yes."

"Good, hurry." He let her think that he had finished, and then took her arms swiftly, gripped them tightly: "Another thing, Violette."

She made no attempt to free herself. "Yes?"

"You haven't lied to me, have you? About anything?"

"I have told you everything I can," she said, and the lift of her chin told of her pride.

"How often were you at the Villa Seblec?"

"Often."

"You didn't live there?"

"Some of the time. Sometimes in a hotel."

"How many other girls lived at the villa?"

"There is Gérard's sister, Raoul's wife," she said. "At times, others visited us, and disappeared. That is all."

He found himself believing her, because he wanted to. She turned away, and seemed to shrug herself into her clothes. He rasped his hand over his stubble, took a drink of water from a carafe, and went into the other bedroom.

The sight of Gérard still shocked him. The absence of Simon and Fifi worried him even more.

When he went back, Violette was ready. She wore a wispy scarf over her head, and a bottle-green suit, which was a little too tight for her.

"What will you do if anything goes wrong with me?" asked Rollison.

"What shall I do?" she echoed. Her lips curved, she smiled with a touch of mockery. "I told you once before, *m'sieu*, that I do not think that I want to live. But you have your business to finish first, and Simon and Fifi have been very kind to me. I would like to help them."

Rollison said: "Why keep talking of dying?"

"It is the good way out."

"The police would certainly like to get you, Violette," said Rollison mildly. "Is it for anything more than you have told me?"

The smile played at her lips.

"No," she said. "And—I did not kill Gérard. I do not kill any of your friends. Do you wish me to follow you, or will you call the police?"

"Follow me, Violette," he said.

He left the house, and as he reached the stairs, saw a little bustling *madame* in the hall. She gaped at sight of a stranger. He ran down the stairs, bowed, murmured: "Madame," politely, and pushed past her into the street. The sun was already warming the morning air. A *gendarme* leaned heavily against the wall of a house opposite; he straightened up sharply when he saw Rollison. Rollison raised a hand in greeting, turned right, and strode towards the main road, the market, and his car.

At the junction of roads near the market, a group of people was held up by a *gendarme* who flashed his baton and shrilled on his whistle, and let trams and lorries rumble by. They were trundling away from the market, having emptied their loads of morning vegetables. A dozen passed; and as they went, Rollison glanced over his shoulder. The policeman who had followed him was just behind; Violette was only a hundred yards away.

He did not go to the car.

He sauntered among the stalls, and no one took much

notice of him. The smell of fresh vegetables and fresh-cut
flowers was like a heavy scent beneath the big iron roofs of
the market. Great piles of cabbages, baskets of beans, onions,
artichokes, leaf spinach, and potatoes were being wheeled on
little trolleys. The cobbled roads were crowded with vans,
mostly with hotel markings on them. Small traders haggled
with farmers who had a site and were trying to get the last
sou for their wares. Only here and there did an old man or an
old woman just sit, silently offering goods for sale, saddened
and bowed down by the hustle and bustle and the ferocity
of the competition. A thousand voices were raised in a
thousand excited shouts, and judging from the way many of
them behaved, they were on the point of violence.

Rollison sauntered through all this.

The policeman followed.

Violette wasn't in sight.

Rollison moved right through the market, past a little
girl who offered him a bunch of roses from a flower-stall
which was near the sea, and then went towards his car.
Panneraude's man moved to a police car, and that told
Rollison how thoroughly they were watching him. He got to
the wheel of the Jaguar, started off, then swung round towards the main part of the town. Suddenly he turned a
corner, trod on the accelerator, and made the car leap forward. He turned two corners on two wheels, then saw a
garage, with a lad outside, at the two yellow pumps. He
turned into the garage, jammed on the brakes, jumped out
and hurried to the lad.

"A back way out, please."

"A back way, *m'sieu*?"

"I am hiding from my friends—a joke, you understand."

"A joke, *m'sieu*!" Young eyes lit up.

The joke and two hundred francs took Rollison to a little
doorway which debouched on to another narrow street. He
took his bearing by the sun, slid down two side streets, and
came upon the market.

There was no sign of his policeman.

He hurried across the road and made for the flower-stall section, searching for Violette. She might have run away. She might have decided that he wouldn't come back. She might have been followed, by brown-skinned men——

She was standing close to one of the market pillars, tall, proud and aloof. When he came up, her eyes brightened; he was sure that she had not felt certain that he would return.

"Hallo, Violette? Ready?"

"Of course."

"Go ahead this time," he said. "I'll follow at a distance. The Café Mulle, not far from the Café Lippe. Once you're in, I'll come in by the side door. Don't ask for me, just ask for the private room."

"Very well," said Violette.

.   .   .   .   .

He followed her, but no one followed him. The ten minutes' walk to the Rue de Sauvant, which ran along the back of the Hotel San Roman, seemed to take hours; every *gendarme* he passed, everyone who looked at him or at the girl, seemed to have some sinister intent; but nothing happened, and he watched her turn into the café.

Three minutes later he entered by a side door.

This was a place he knew well, and he had come to an arrangement with Papa Mulle, to take messages for him. He could rely on the old man who owned the café.

Well, he thought he could.

The café itself was dark. Two or three people were sitting at glass-topped tables, sharing coffee and rolls with advertisements for wines, vermouths, and cigarettes. Mulle's eldest grandson, Jean, was behind the little counter; a bright-eyed youth. He pointed towards the door which led to a small private room.

So Violette was there.

Rollison brushed aside the tapestry curtain which hung in the doorway, then stepped inside.

Violette wasn't alone.

Fifi was with her.

20

TRAP OR TRUTH?

FIFI was very pale, and looked as if she had not slept. Her hair was pathetically untidy. She watched Rollison coming in, her eyes lack-lustre. It was obvious that she had been crying; little dry tracks of tears showed on her shiny skin. Sitting there with coffee, rolls, and butter in front of her, she looked a round dumpling of a woman.

Jean appeared at the doorway.

"Petit déjeuner, m'sieu?"

"In ten minutes, Jean, please," Rollison said. "Close the door."

He waited until he heard it close, and drew nearer to Fifi. Violette was leaning against the wall, one hand at the V of her blouse, playing with a brooch which glinted in the one electric light. Go to Montmartre, to the *demi-monde* of any city of France, and you would find women leaning against a wall like that, as if defying not only men, but the world.

"What is it, Fifi?" asked Rollison.

She made herself speak.

"You were right," she said in a toneless voice. "We should have gone back to Paris, but we would not listen to you. That is one good thing: you cannot blame yourself for what has happened to Simon, can you?"

The tonelessness touched her words with horror.

"What has happened?" Rollison asked stiffly.

"They have taken him," Fifi said. She rested her hands on the glass-topped table, and Rollison saw them clenching and unclenching. "It was because of Gérard. *How I hate Gérard*," she went on savagely.

Had Gérard been alive, he would have been in danger then.

Could Fifi speak of him like that if she knew that the lad was dead?

"What happened?" Rollison asked again.

"Simon made one simple little discovery. I do not know what it was at first. He refused to tell me. He said——" Fifi seemed to flinch, fists and body cringed as if some pain stabbed through her. "He said that the knowledge was too dangerous for me to have, and he would keep it for himself. He was going to tell you, and met Gérard near your hotel room. Simon had gone to see you, and you were not there. Gérard went with us. He had to hide, because after he had failed to take you prisoner from your hotel he was too frightened to go back to the Villa Seblec. Men who had followed Gérard found him with Simon. Simon tried to see you; it was after you had left the Count at dinner, perhaps while I was talking to you. Then Gérard and Simon were *forced* to go away with two men. I do not know how, but he went. I returned to the *pension*, not knowing what had happened, and Simon telephoned me and told me all this. Someone was standing over him with a gun or a knife, he said. I was to leave the *pension*, and stay somewhere else. They were orders, and I—I obeyed them."

Tears began to fall.

"Did he say why?"

"No," Fifi said, "no. But I could guess, or I believed I could guess. I thought that they wanted to kill Violette. I thought if I let them, they might not hurt Simon. So I left her."

"Was Gérard in your room?" Rollison demanded.

"He was not," said Fifi, through clenched teeth. "If ever I see the beast again, I——"

Violette looked at Rollison; she hadn't moved. Fifi had deserted her, but who could blame Fifi?

And why had Violette been left alone at the *pension*? Had the men of the Villa Seblec changed their minds about wanting her dead?

He brushed the question aside.

"I came here because I knew you would come sooner or later," Fifi went on. She sounded choky. "You remember the first time we met in Nice? It was in the Café Mulle. I will tell you another thing. Here in this room Simon began his career, here he received his first payment. Here——" She broke off, fighting back tears.

"Do you know anything to help us find him?" Rollison asked, and made himself sound calm. "Have you any idea why they took him away, or what it is that he knows?"

She said: "I think he knows who Chicot is."

.   .   .   .   .

For the first time since Rollison had been in the back room, Violette moved. She took a few steps forwards, pulled up a chair, and sat down. Close to Fifi, she looked at her with infinite sympathy.

"He knows who Chicot is," Violette said, "and I would recognise Chicot if I saw him. So both of us are to be killed." Her hand touched Fifi's, but she looked up at Rollison. "Unless you have some good idea to save us, *m'sieu*." There was bitterness but no mockery in her tone. "Chicot is not M. le Comte. He is not Raoul. He is not Dr. Morency. Certainly he is not Sautot. He is very anxious not to be found out, isn't he? It would be interesting to know why?"

"All trails lead to Chicot," Rollison said softly. "Everyone blames Chicot. Gérard made a statement that involved him. I think Gérard died because he knew Chicot, but Chicot is just a name."

"Gérard *is* dead?" Fifi looked up sharply.

"Killed, Fifi," Rollison said. He didn't say where the youth's body was; or that when the police found it, they would be on the look-out for them all. "Know Chicot and die. Know Chicot——"

He broke off.

The door from the café opened, and little Jean came in, carrying a tray with fresh coffee, croissants, butter, and a white dish of marmalade. Behind him came Papa Mulle himself.

Mulle was an old man now. There had been a time when he had been called the Father of All Clowns, but nothing in his expression or his face suggested that as he came in. He was almost bald, and the fringe of hair at his temples was snowy white; so were his eyebrows and his moustache. But he had a fresh complexion and eyes almost as bright as Jean's, his grandson's, and his step was sprightly. He came with both hands extended to greet Rollison, and he did not seem to notice any tension in the air. His smile encompassed Fifi and Violette, but his interest was only in the Toff.

"To see you again, my friend, is one of the pleasures of living! I wish you had come later in the day; we could have opened a bottle in your honour. Tonight, perhaps, or another night?" He stopped pumping Rollison's hands. "You look very well. Are you?"

"Fine, Papa, fine."

"Oh, there is doubtless something in being an Englishman," Mulle said off-handedly. "Did I hear you speaking of Chicot?"

"Do you know Chicot?" Fifi burst out.

Papa Mulle looked at her with mild surprise.

"But of course I knew Chicot, as we all did. Even M. Rollison has seen Chicot, the master of us all. Poor Chicot!

He died in poverty; everyone is aware of that. He died a bitter man also, betrayed by his friends. Perhaps betrayed is too strong a word," went on Papa Mulle sadly, "but not to Chicot. There were seven men who were to finance his great dream: a theatre of his own, in Paris, in London, and in New York. One of them betrayed Chicot's only daughter, and she killed herself. In his bitterness and despair, Chicot could think of nothing else. He lost his magic, and they all deserted him. His friends disappeared, he died unloved and deserted. Poor Chicot," Papa Mulle said softly, and raised his hands and sighed. "It is said that he had a son, but no one has ever seen him."

Violette breathed: "A son for Chicot?"

"A son!" gasped Fifi.

"Is there so surprising in having a son?" demanded the old man mildly.

"No," said Rollison, "or even a grandson, Papa Mulle. Or friends. What was the name of the man who ran off with Chicot's daughter?"

Papa Mulle said:

"You may know, I suppose. It is an old, old business now, the first of the many *affaires* of M. le Comte de Vignolles. You are not surprised?"

"No," said Rollison softly. "Not at all surprised. Are you strong enough to be given a shock?"

Mulle looked startled. "Strong enough to——" He broke off, and chuckled. "It will take much more than a shock to harm me, my friend. Try it."

"Simon Leclair is in grave danger," Rollison said abruptly. "So are other friends of mine. I can't be sure; but I think M. le Comte de Vignolles could help to remove the danger."

Papa Mulle did not speak.

"One way to find out is to talk to M. le Comte," went on Rollison dryly, "but on my ground, not his. Can you find me some helpers, lend me two cars, and also find me a place where I can talk to him?"

The coldness faded from Mulle's eyes; they grew warm until eventually they glowed.

"Yes, my friend, I can," he said.

.   .   .   .

M. le Comte de Vignolles was in the library of his villa, which was built on the hills overlooking the sea, between the middle and upper corniche from Monte Carlo to Nice. He was alone. The room was large, but the most striking feature was the huge window, stretching the whole width of one wall, and overlooking the promontory which jutted into the sea at Cap Mirabeau and the Ile de Seblec. It was often said that his villa had the finest views in France.

He was writing.

Some movement caught his eye, and he saw a car turn into the drive off the corniche road. It made him frown, for it was a gleaming cream-coloured car, and he did not recognise it. He was not expecting strangers. He shrugged his shoulders and tried to put it out of his mind, but it would not go. When a tap came at the door, he said at once:

"Yes, come in."

A middle-aged man dressed in black entered.

"M. le Comte, an English gentleman, one M. Rollison, asks if you will be good enough to see him."

"*Who?*"

"An English gentleman, M. ——"

"Beautifully said," said Rollison, and startled the flunkey by appearing behind him. He put him gently to one side, and entered the room. "Good morning, good morning. My, what a view!" He moved across to the window and stood looking out, marvelling. "Wonderful! What a lucky man you are."

"M. le Comte," said the servant tautly, "is it your wish to have M. Rollison shown out?"

"Shown or thrown, they scan at home," said Rollison brightly. "But I don't think that my host will be as unkind as that. Circumstances have changed. Will you leave us to talk together?"

The servant said: "In one moment, M. le Comte, I can call Charles and Paul. Together they——"

"Wait outside," de Vignolles said abruptly.

"As you wish, m'sieu."

"But they can come and throw you out at the touch of a switch," de Vignolles said to Rollison. The anger in his eyes might have been there since the previous night. There was disquiet, too; a sense of fear. "What do you want?"

"Some friends of mine," said Rollison promptly. "Simon Leclair, known as the natural successor to the original Chicot; Daphne Myall, just the daughter of an unhappy woman, and a few other daughters. Not very much, after all."

"You must be mad! To come here and talk to me and——"

"Burble," said Rollison brightly. "I agree with you. In your position I would be angry, too. But there isn't anything you can do about it now, for you're in trouble. You're in *big* trouble. You see, I think you know who Chicot is. I think he blackmails you into helping him, perhaps into providing these pretty girls. You hoped I would trace and kill Chicot. You dare not name him, but you thought a thousand pounds would make me keener to find out who he is. Well, you're going to name him, M. le Comte."

"I do not know him!"

"I don't believe you. Send him a message, will you? That I'm prepared to keep away from the police and give him time to get away, provided Simon Leclair and the girls are freed."

"It isn't true," de Vignolles said shrilly. "I do not know who Chicot is!"

Rollison grinned.

"Chicot, son of Chicot," he declared. "Bright idea, too. Lure the girls down here with bright lights, turn their heads, use them as decoys to fleece wealthy old fools, then keep them prisoner, use them as the bait in more big swindles. When they're guilty of that, they're in Chicot's hands. Villa Seblec is kept as a kind of home from home for the young ladies until they can't stand the confinement any longer, and 'volunteer' to go to the African coast. Wealthy sheiks like pretty white ladies, no? Violette Monet was an exception, because Chicot fell in love with her."

He paused. Then:

"Who *is* Chicot?"

"I do not know!" cried de Vignolles.

Rollison felt quite sure that he did; quite sure that he lived in terror of Chicot, and dared not name him.

"M. le Comte, what would happen if I were to tell Morency or Raoul, at the Villa Seblec, that you have named him?" Rollison inquired mildly.

"No!" cried de Vignolles.

"He wouldn't be surprised, as we dined together."

De Vignolles was sweating, and breathing in short gasps; a frightened man. A little more pressure, and he would crack; but Rollison did not want him to crack here.

The manservant was at the door.

The Toff relaxed, as the door opened, and touched his forehead lightly.

"*Au revoir*," he beamed, and flicked a card towards the desk so dexterously that it lay on the blotting-pad on which de Vignolles had been writing. "My card." He bowed, moved to the door, and went out.

De Vignolles saw him chuck the manservant under the chin.

De Vignolles did not close the door, but stared after the Englishman, who moved lightly as a ballet-dancer and who suddenly began to sing a *risqué* song in rich Paris argot.

Then he disappeared.

Ten minutes later, M. le Comte de Vignolles left his villa in a chauffeur-driven Cadillac, an exquisite sea-green in colour, and was taken safely to the drive and on to the main road. A few hundred yards along, round a corner, the driver was forced to slow down. Workmen were blocking half the road, and a car was coming towards them on the other half. De Vignolles glared at the driver of this, who looked a very old man in beret and blouse. The man was swearing at his engine, which was at least as venerable as he was himself.

His engine had stalled.

De Vignolles opened his mouth to say something excessively unpleasant; and closed it again. Two of the workmen had turned towards him and the Cadillac. A man suddenly appeared from the side of the road, and pulled open his door.

The chauffeur exclaimed: "*Nom d'un nom*, get away from here!"

Then he saw the gun in the other man's hand.

.   .   .   .   .

"You can't want to move more quickly than I do," said Rollison earnestly. "Take off your hat and coat—and hurry!"

The chauffeur gulped, and de Vignolles started to speak, but bit on the words. He looked dreadful. The chauffeur took off his hat and coat, and one of the 'workmen' hurried towards him and put them on; the other forced the chauffeur to climb out.

Rollison got in next to de Vignolles.

"Drive on, my man," said he grandiloquently; "you know our destination." He turned to de Vignolles, and rested a hand lightly on his arm. "And don't you wish you did?"

De Vignolles was trembling violently.

Obviously he didn't like the knife in Rollison's hand.

F

21

HOSTAGE

AT a lonely spot on the road between Nice and Cannes, they reached some cross-roads, and slowed down. De Vignolles had hardly uttered a word on the journey. Rollison glanced round at him, and saw that his face was almost colourless, that his eyes had the sick look which fear could give to a man.

Gérard had had the same kind of fear.

They drove towards the back of the towns, and turned off the main road. Soon the country was broken and untidy, and the grass was burned more yellow than green. A few fruit-trees looked listless in the sun. Big, circular hay-stacks cast huge shadows. Two oxen, pulling an ancient plough with a woman in a huge sun-bonnet behind it, plodded noisily through the sun-baked earth. Then they came to a hill and, on the other side, took another narrow lane which led to a small farmhouse.

A few chickens scratched; a pig grunted. Hanging on either side of the small doorway were three pairs of coloured *sabots*. Tobacco hung from the top of two barns, being cured in the sun. The farmyard smell was potent, and de Vignolles seemed to find his nostrils twitching without any command or effort of will.

The car turned through the open gateway and stopped in front of the house itself. It was narrow and tall, with plaster walls and a pink wash which hadn't been renewed for several years.

"Home again," said Rollison brightly. "Quite a change, isn't it? Mind you step high when you get out; we didn't think to bring your valet."

"Rollison——"

"Out," said Rollison, and took his wrist. "Now." He pulled, and de Vignolles grunted, then stepped out quickly. "De Vignolles," went on Rollison in a hard voice, "you may be a Count. You may be a millionaire. You may have powerful friends." He paused, and then pointed to a pig-stye, where a huge sow was grunting and muzzling. "Do you see that pig?"

De Vignolles licked his lips.

"I'd give tomorrow's bacon more consideration than you," Rollison said, and he sounded as if he meant it. "The farm is owned by friends of mine. No one will hear any noise you make. You can scream from now until next Monday, and no one who matters will hear. Understand?"

"What is it—you want?"

"Chicot," said Rollison. "Remember?"

He let de Vignolles go, and turned towards the open front door. Violette was just inside. He didn't see Fifi, although he knew that she was here somewhere. Violette gave him a lazy smile, and looked at de Vignolles as if he were something that crawled.

The room into which Rollison stepped was large and poorly lit. Some big old-fashioned chairs stood about, a large table with a red chenille table-cloth on it, a sofa, two big oil-lamps. The floor was bare, but looked as if it had been recently scrubbed.

De Vignoles was thrust in, behind Rollison. He had hardly spoken a word. His pallor was greater, and green-tinged, now. His lips moved, and his tongue showed before he closed his mouth.

Violette looked at him with that same supercilious expression when he glanced at her, as if imploring help.

In the large fireplace there was a wooden rocking-chair.

"Sit down," said Rollison, and when he Vignolles hesitated, he took his wrists and thrust him into it. The chair rocked backwards alarmingly; de Vignolles thought that it was going to tip over. He panicked and tried to get up, fell back, cried out; and gave his head a sickening bang on the back of the chair.

The chair steadied.

"The few that are brave," said Rollison bleakly. "Listen to me, de Vignolles. You're so scared of Chicot that you do what he tells you. You saw me because he told you to. You were to offer me a thousand pounds, and I was to tell you what I knew about Chicot.

"You probably want him dead.

"You daren't let him or his men realise that you do. You daren't name him, but—you *will*. When I came to see you, you wanted to get help, and instructions. You could not telephone, so planned to see—*whom*?"

"No!" cried de Vignolles.

"Ask him first," said Fifi from a doorway, "is Simon dead or alive?"

.   .   .   .   .

She moved towards the Frenchman. Her hands were empty, and her arms hung by her side. Her little plump body looked shrunken in a blue overall. Her hair was still untidy, and she hadn't put on any lipstick or rouge. The deadliness which terrified the Frenchman was in her eyes. Rollison saw it, and knew that if ever a woman stepped towards him as she was moving towards de Vignolles, he would also feel afraid.

De Vignolles tried to get up. The chair rocked. He licked his lips again, grabbed the arms as if to steady himself, but only made it move more rapidly.

"Is he alive or dead?" asked Fifi very softly.

"I do not know!" de Vignolles sobbed. "That I swear to you."

"If he is dead," Fifi said, "I shall kill you, M. le Comte." The sneer in the way she uttered that title must have made the Frenchman writhe. "Where is Simon?"

"He—I do not know!"

"Where is he?"

"If you know you'd better talk," Rollison advised. "Fifi really wants to know. She was in the Resistance during the war, and learned a lot of tricks, especially on how to use scissors. You wouldn't want that kind of face-lifting, would you!"

"*Keep her away!*" screeched de Vignolles.

"I *could* use a whip," Rollison said musingly. There was one hanging by the fireplace, a bullock's whip with several knotted ends to the leather thongs. He went towards it. "A very pretty thing. Who is Chicot?"

"I do not know!"

Fifi stood watching, but Violette had turned away, and was looking out of the window. No one stirred outside, except the old sow, which kept grunting and pushing against the rotting fence which surrounded her. Chickens scratched. The men who had come with Rollison were at the back of the farm, out of sight and hearing.

Rollison had a strange feeling.

It was nearly over; this man would crack very soon. He must have been living on fear for months; perhaps for years. His bluster and his arrogance had been built on the shifting sands of fear, and they were crumbling fast. His hands would not keep still.

He almost squealed.

"I do not know Chicot, but I know what he does. Please take that woman away. I will tell you all I can."

"Hurry, and never mind the woman."

De Vignolles gulped.

"Years ago I—I killed a man, an accident, you understand, but Chicot found out. I had—I had known his sister, he——"

"We know, you can skip that," Rollison said.

The man's face worked.

"So, Chicot blackmailed me, for many years. Then he went away, I became rich—until he returned. I had the

Baccarat, much money, everything and—Chicot began again. I was to have—to have some girls come to the *Baccarat*, made drunk, and—and go to the Villa with certain men. You understand? Afterwards, I did not see them again. That— *that is all I know!*"

Rollison said stonily:

"Who is Chicot?"

"I swear I do not know!"

"What happens to the girls?"

"How can I tell?"

"Must I use the whip?"

"I do not know Chicot," babbled de Vignolles, "but I am told he will be at the Villa Seblec tonight. I am to see him there, but he will be disguised. And—and more things, I can tell you. I have threatened to tell the police, to confess all; and what does he say? If the Villa is raided, if the police go, then there will be a great explosion!" His eyes looked wild; glaring. "I do not lie to you. The girls are hidden deep in the cliff, and there is a powerful charge of dynamite under the place. They will be buried, no one will know how it happened. Already there are some pieces of an old bomb on the cliff; it will look like the explosion of a bomb dropped years ago by a crippled aircraft. Believe me, they will all be killed. That is how Chicot plans."

De Vignolles stopped, and silence followed. It lasted, heavy and menacing, for a long time. Then Rollison said slowly:

"Where is the dynamite?"

A sharp, explosive sound outside cut across his words. It made him break off, made the others turn swiftly, even the Frenchman looked towards the window.

Fifi cried out.

Rollison saw one of Papa Mulle's men fall full length in the muck of the yard.

A small, brown-clad, brown-skinned man appeared at the doorway, knife in hand.

The knife flashed.

De Vignolles's scream was cut off when the blade entered his chest.

22

THE WORD OF A DYING MAN

THE rocking-chair went to and fro, to and fro, while the echoes of the scream faded; the rockers of the chair scraped a little on the stone floor. The blade was buried in de Vignolles' breast, on the left side; a little of the steel showed. His hands were cupped close to the handle, but did not touch it. His mouth was wide open.

The brown-skinned man moved from the doorway, swift as a flash of light.

Rollison moved after him, and saw one of Papa Mulle's friends running. Rollison stopped, and swung round. Even if they caught the Arab there was no certainty that he could talk to help them. Somewhere under the cliff near the Villa Seblec were those helpless girls; and de Vignolles knew about them, and might know how to get them out.

Fifi was standing close to the Count, one hand raised, as if she could not believe that this had happened.

Violette was saying:

"What can we do for him? What can we *do*."

"Get water, towels. Hurry!" Fifi suddenly became a moving bundle, and swung round.

In fact, there wasn't a thing they could do.

Rollison knew, and de Vignolles knew. For the first time since they had met they eyed each other as equals, and without any measure of pretence. The expression in de

Vignolles's eyes was different. He was not afraid. That was the startling thing: the fear had gone.

His lips moved.

"Get me—a priest," he whispered. "As you are a man, send for a priest."

Rollison said quietly: "Violette, talk to the men, find out where the nearest priest is, and send for him. Or go and fetch him. Hurry, please."

The girl looked at de Vignolles with a strange expression, then turned and hurried out of the shadowy room. Fifi was in the wash-house, next door. Rollison and this man were alone together, and Rollison knew that there was little time left. Minutes? He couldn't be sure. There was not much bleeding, but if that blade were withdrawn, blood might flow swiftly. Now it was internal. If he pulled the blade out, then the bleeding might kill de Vignolles on the instant.

The Frenchman lowered his hands, very slowly.

"Thank you," he whispered.

"She will hurry," Rollison said. "Do you know who Chicot is?"

"I—I do not know. I am—am given orders by Morency. Twice—twice I have seen Chicot, always in disguise—as Mephisto, you understand, as—Mephisto."

"*Are* there girl prisoners at the Villa Seblec?"

"Yes." The tone of de Vignolles's voice was so weak that Rollison could hardly hear. His lips moved slowly, painfully. "Yes, there are—prisoners. Young—women. In the cliff, behind—the Villa. But——"

He gave a funny little cough.

Fifi came in, carrying a bowl of water which slopped over the side, and a towel draped on her arm. She missed a step. Rollison did not look round at her, but felt sure that she had realised that no ministrations could help to save the dying man.

De Vignolles's eyes closed, his lips moved as if he were

trying to drink. Fifi seized a glass, filled it with water, and put it to his lips. Her hands were shaky.

"A spoon," said Rollison quietly.

She hurried off to get one.

De Vignolles opened his eyes, waveringly. The light seemed to hurt them. He moved his right hand, and Rollison put out his own, to take the Frenchman's; already the flesh felt cold.

"Do not take—police," de Vignolles said. "If the police go, they will—be——" He gulped, opened his mouth again, made that strange, haunting little noise. Fifi, close at hand, put a spoon of water to his lips. He felt that it was there, the tip of his tongue showed for a moment, seeking the moisture. "Be—blown up," he went on. "Buried alive, in—in the cliff. Do not raid—do not attempt to—to rescue them by——"

He stopped again.

This time he did not notice when the spoonful of water was close to his lips. It was a long time before he tried to speak; then the words came as a whisper.

"Do not use force," he said; "do not use force."

He fell silent, and then moved spasmodically, gripped Rollison's hands with startling strength, and cried:

"Father! Father!"

Outside, there were no sounds.

Inside, there was only Fifi's heavy breathing.

"Is he—is he dead?" she asked, in a hushed voice.

"Not quite dead," Rollison said. He shifted his position, and in doing so made the rocking-chair move. It looked ludicrous; a big, handsome man sitting there with the blade of the knife protruding from his chest, rocking to and fro, to and fro, with his eyes closed and his mouth slightly open.

But he was breathing.

He was still breathing, although each breath was very shallow, when Violette returned with the priest from a nearby village.

Papa Mulle's men had caught the Arab, a lithe, brown, frightened man with jet-black eyes, nervous movements, and hands which wouldn't keep still. He did not speak English, but his French was as fluent as a native of France, and he was eager to talk.

He had been told to kill de Vignolles, he said, and had seen him in the car. So he followed the tyre-tracks here, and carried out his orders.

Why?

He was employed to carry out such orders, by men whose names he did not know. He stayed at a small house near the Villa Seblec. He sometimes served on board a ship; the ship sometimes carried white girls to Algiers——

He swore that he knew nothing of the Villa Seblec, or the hiding-place under the cliff.

"Did anyone else at the Villa Seblec know of this farm?"

"No. I was alone," he said.

"What shall we do with him?" Mulle's men asked.

"For the time being, leave him here," said Rollison. He turned to Fifi. "I'm going into Nice. Will you stay here or come with me? I think you'd be safer here, and certainly I'd be happier."

"Is there something I can do to help in Nice?"

"No," Rollison assured her, "nothing at all, Fifi."

She shrugged, and agreed to stay. She seemed very lonely, and more than a little frightened. The death of de Vignolles had shocked her; in fact, death itself had shocked her. She was without her Simon, and did not know what to do. Rollison, studying her, wondered what she would feel like if Simon were to die; if he *were* to be blown up.

Would that happen?

Would a dying man lie?

Rollison didn't know the answer, but he doubted it. Faced with death, de Vignolles had almost certainly told the truth. Somewhere inside the cliff, behind or near the Villa Seblec, there was the hiding-place where the girls were held.

If the police raided the Villa, or if anyone raided it in force, there was grave risk of that explosion, of them being buried alive.

Face it.

"What is there that I can do?" Violette asked.

Rollison looked at her, broodingly.

"You can come with me to Nice," he said, and added very quietly: "And I may ask you to give yourself up at the Villa Seblec. That's one way that we might be able to save the others."

Violette simply shrugged.

. . . . .

Rollison drove back to Nice.

He did not know the way, but all signposts, even those at tiny crossroads, pointed to the town.

Violette sat silent.

Rollison kept turning over the possibilities in his mind, and glanced at her occasionally, wondered what she was thinking. She had that strange, aloof courage, a kind of fatalism. She was prepared to die, and had been sure for some time that she would die soon.

So, she would take any risk.

He did not have to take risks with her, but—there were the others. Little Daphne Myall, and others like her; and Simon. He tried to make himself feel sure that Simon was in the same desperate plight, but at heart he wasn't sure.

Did Fifi suspect that Simon had betrayed him?

He said roughly: "Violette."

"Yes?"

"I don't know if I made it clear. The girls are in that chamber somewhere in the hillside. If the Villa is raided, it'll be blown up and the girls will be buried alive. So the Villa mustn't be raided by force. You and I have to manage this between us."

"Why not?" she said.

"It's a big risk for us both. But if you let them catch you and take you back, you can keep them busy while I come along. Will you take a chance?"

"I have told you that I will," she said. "But how can I allow them to catch me, without showing that it is a trick?"

"We'll find a way," said Rollison. "Go to the Café Lippe, which Chicot's men will be watching. I'll come for you there or send a message." His foot stabbed down on the accelerator. "And I'll get you out of the jam," he promised.

Just words?

.   .   .   .   .

"Well, if that is the case, then I believe you," Panneraude said. He was in his office, unshaven, tired. "The Count was dying?" He shrugged. "Then he did not lie. So, what do I arrange? First, to send two men to the Café Lippe, to inquire for Violette Monet. That is easy. Then, to have her followed, but not caught. Good. And then——" He looked down at some notes he had made on a pad. "Some men at sea, in dinghies, close to the jetty at the Villa Seblec. When you give the signal, we shall raid. Is that right?"

Rollison said: "It's exactly right."

"I still think that I shall be sending a sad message to your friends at Scotland Yard," said Panneraude, "but this we shall have to try. What signal will you give?"

"A whistle," Rollison said. He put his fingers to his lips, and drew a deep breath, but before he could utter a sound, Panneraude was on his feet. "Enough! One, two, three?"

"One ought to be quite enough," said Rollison very grimly.

23

THE MAN WHOM ROLLISON KNEW

THE water was warm.

Rollison swam steadily towards the jetty of the Villa Seblec. He had a waterproof bag fastened round his waist, with the oddments of clothing and the gun and the knife he knew he would need. He made hardly a sound. He knew that the police dinghies were as close inshore as they dared come; it was a moonlight night, and if they came too close, they might be seen.

He reached the jetty.

Had the police raided the Villa from here they would have talked among themselves, and the sounds would have been heard over the loud-speaker system inside. That would have given Morency and the others all the warning they needed.

He would make no sound; he must make none.

He climbed up the steps.

He crouched low, moved along the jetty, and found the first path of shade, behind a clump of bougainvillea. He rubbed himself down quickly, then slid into shorts and a pair of rubber-soled shoes. The small automatic was in the pocket of the shorts, and a sheathed knife was fastened inside the waist-band.

He moved cautiously until he could see the back of the Villa and the narrow road which led from it. Two or three cars passed along the main road; their headlights appeared and as quickly disappeared.

Another car approached from Nice.

He heard it change gear, and a few seconds later knew that it was coming along the private road. He kept in the shadows of the walls. The front of the house was floodlit, but not the back or sides.

The car pulled up.

He heard the mutter of voices, then the sounds of men getting out of the car; then a rough curse, and:

"Make her come."

There was a pause: men grunted: then in the dim light, Rollison saw Violette dragged out of the car. He watched as they pushed her towards the back door. One of them opened it with a key, the other pushed her inside.

"I shall put the car away," the second man said.

"Yes. Hurry."

The man who had opened the door turned round. Violette was out of sight, with the second man. Rollison moved swiftly, to the side of the car. The man got in, reversed, and then swung into the garage, which took four cars. He did not give a thought to danger.

Rollison was waiting at the end of the garage. The man came, whistling. Rollison let him pass, then shot out a hand and clutched his neck.

The cry was strangled on the night air. The man kicked, struggled, and fell silent.

Rollison dragged him into the garage, tied him up with a length of cord from his pocket, stuffed a handkerchief into his mouth. Then he went to the house.

The door wasn't locked.

There would be microphones here and elsewhere; he dared not make a sound. The lights were on. He heard no noise at all, but knew that the women servants were almost certainly in the kitchen. The tour he had made the previous night helped greatly now. He slipped past the kitchen door. A radio was tuned in to dance-music, which came softly. There was no sign or sound of the man, or of Violette.

Rollison went towards the room of satyrs. He saw that a door was open, and white light came through. He drew nearer, making no sound.

Raoul was saying: "I'll make her talk."

That was all.

Rollison went nearer still, but couldn't see inside. He was near enough to hear the *sss-sss-sss* of Morency's hands. He didn't think about that; he didn't really think about Violette at that moment. There were the other girls, not far from here; and at the touch of a switch they could be buried alive, buried without trace.

And Simon?

Morency said: "Didn't your fine friend Rollison save you from the police, after all?"

"I was to meet him at the Café Lippe," she said. "He did not come, the police came instead." She sounded as if she were frightened beyond all words. "Don't—don't hurt me again, please don't hurt me."

"We shall hurt you again," Raoul said, "whenever you tell us a lie. What happened at the farm this afternoon? Did de Vignolles die?"

She caught her breath.

"Yes."

Rollison heard a movement, followed by another gasp. He couldn't see but could guess what had happened; Raoul had snatched at her wrist. The brute in the youth would always be close to the surface.

"Did de Vignolles talk first?"

"No!"

"Tell me the truth. Did he talk?"

"*No!*"

"Did he name Chicot?"

"Please let me go, let me go," she sobbed; and Rollison knew that nothing would have persuaded her to beg like that except the fact that she was trying to help him; and to help the others. So she sank her pride. "Please let me go!"

"Did de Vignolles name Chicot?"

"*No!*" she screamed. "He said he did not know who he was!"

"Wait one moment, Raoul," said Morency. "Let me see whether a little hot tobacco will persuade her to tell the truth. Violette, my dear, did the late lamented Count tell Rollison——"

"He was killed, he didn't say a word!" Violette cried.

"I wonder if we can believe her," murmured Morency. "Perhaps we had better assume that she is telling the truth, for the time being. Chicot will soon be here, and he would like to question her himself, I'm sure. Don't you think so, Violette? Don't you look forward to seeing Chicot again?"

"No," she gasped. "No, not Chicot; he——"

"The wages of treachery are pain and fear, my dear," said Morency. "Raoul, take Violette along to the *salon*." He gave a little giggle. "The small *salon*; she isn't to mix with the others, yet."

There was a moment's pause, before Violette exclaimed, as if in a fresh access of fear. Rollison went closer to the door. He peered in, and saw the hole appearing in the floor. It was at the spot where Morency had stood for so long the previous night—a large, rectangular hole.

Raoul and the other man pushed Violette towards it. She stepped down on to steps which were invisible to Rollison. One after the other, they disappeared. Morency looked at the hole, and Rollison saw it gradually closing; a panel slid into position, and blotted it right out.

There was only one faint sound now. *Sss-sss-sss*.

Rollison moistened his lips as he went forward. He opened the door wider. Morency was standing and looking at one of the little statuettes—and might almost have been looking at his own image. His back was towards Rollison. Rollison stepped right into the room. Perhaps there was a button to push, a way in which Morency could warn the others if the alarm were raised too quickly.

Two yards separated them.

Morency turned slowly——

Rollison moved, hands shooting out. There was time for Morency to open his mouth, but none for him to shout. Rollison's fingers closed round his neck. He writhed for a moment, his eyes seemed to pop out of his head, but no sound came.

Then Rollison gradually slackened his hold. Morency gasped, and turned his head from side to side, tried to cringe away. Rollison held him by one arm; and all the fear that Violette had had of Raoul was nothing to the fear which this old man had of Rollison.

Any man, looking upon Rollison then, would have understood his terror.

"No," muttered Morency. "No, don't kill me; don't kill me, I beg you!"

Rollison said: "I'll break your bones one by one, Morency, if you don't tell me where the girls are, and where the detonating switch is. Tell me—now."

Morency was shivering, with the fear of death very close. Sweat smeared his forehead in glistening globules, and his mouth would not keep steady. He tried to point with his free arm, towards the spot where the hole in the floor had been.

"You go—you go down there. Walk—walk for twenty metres or more, and—and you come to a door. This—this door will open if you touch the black mark at—at one side. It is there for anyone to see, just a small black mark. Inside there will be—there will be Raoul and—and Violette. In the next rooms, all the others.

"I am telling you the truth!" Morency suddenly screamed.

"Part of the truth. Where is the switch?"

"I—I do not know, I——"

"Morency," said Rollison very softly, "you won't save your life by pretending ignorance. I'll kill you now, if you don't tell me where that switch is."

No one could have doubted that he meant exactly what he said.

Morency whispered. "It is—it is above the doorway below—below there. Look." He moved towards one of the statues. His left hand went out. Rollison gritted his teeth, knowing that the man might be trying to fool him, that whatever he was going to do might be deadly. Morency trembled so violently that he looked as if he were going to collapse.

He touched the cloven hoof of a statuette.

There was a moment of silence; then a soft, sliding noise. The hole appeared in the floor. Morency went towards it, his feet tapping on the floor itself. He pointed. Rollison, crouching, could see the steps which led towards a doorway, and, above the doorway, a switch. It was so very ordinary; just an electric-light switch set in a plastic surround, and above the door.

"That is it," breathed Morency.

"Is there another?"

"No! No, I swear——"

He didn't finish; it wasn't necessary for him to say another word. Rollison felt certain that he was telling the truth.

The switch was within reach. He could dismantle it. He could make quite sure that the horror which Morency, Raoul and the still unknown Chicot were prepared to bring upon the girls below the cliffs need never happen. First, deal with Morency, then find tools, then——

He turned swiftly upon Morency.

The terror which leapt into the little man's eyes almost called for pity. He feared just one thing: death. Rollison did not plan to kill him; there was no need. He snapped a clenched fist at Morency's chin, felt the jolt, saw the head go back, and the eyes roll. It was swift, decisive, sufficient. He stopped Morency from falling. He would be out for several minutes, time to bind him hand and foot, make sure that when he came round he could do no harm.

There were the servants, too.

And little time.

Rollison lowered Morency to the floor, and turned towards the door; and stopped.

Hope oozed out of him.

He had not heard a sound. Nothing had warned him, nothing given him the slightest cause for alarm. But a man stood there. He knew, at that first startled, bewildering glimpse, that this was Chicot. He *knew*. Here was the man who had organised all this, the man who could plan with utter ruthlessness, who could kill, and warp, and hate.

And he, the Toff, knew this man as a friend.

.   .   .   .   .

It was not Leclair.

It was Rambeau, the Night Club King, the man whose help he had sought when he had first planned to visit Nice.

Rambeau, *alias* Chicot, stood there smiling; and the gun in his right hand fed the smile with menace.

24

CHICOT

RAMBEAU'S smile broadened, very slowly.

He was rather a stocky man with broad shoulders and a broad face, but ordinary enough. There was just a hint of rugged handsomeness about him, and a hint of recklessness in his expression. He looked very sure of himself, and he had good cause to be.

The Toff did not move.

"My dear friend Rollison," Rambeau said, "you have done very well to get so far. I was afraid that you would; that is why I came so quickly. I decided that it was wise to make quite sure that no one who can connect me with Chicot could talk about it to the police." He spread his one free hand, but didn't move the gun. "I am sure you understand that it would be most unfortunate. Much better that this phase in my activities should end now, don't you agree?" His smile became almost gay. "It has worked very well; I am an extremely rich man. In future I shall be able to give the very best in my clubs, the supreme artistes of Europe. And America; yes, why not America? And you, my friend—you did not guess. Something your servant said made me think that you did; that is why I hurried, why I sent orders to kill you. But you are so utterly surprised, you could not have suspected me for one moment."

The Toff said: "No, Chicot, I didn't."

"Always so truthful," marvelled Rambeau. "That is one of the things that I admire so much in you. Truthfulness and good looks, eh? And good luck! But eventually the good luck has to come to an end."

"What did Jolly say?" asked Rollison steadily. "What made you think I knew?"

"He said that he was sure that you were on the point of success."

Rollison winced.

Yes, Jolly had told him he had said that, to Rambeau—to *Chicot*. No irony could be greater, none could hurt more.

"So——" Rambeau shrugged. "I fly here, and find out what is happening. It is decided to create another Chicot, to have someone whom de Vignolles and others can blame as the villain. I was to tell de Vignolles to name him. Who, do you ask?"

He was grinning.

"Who but your old friend Simon Leclair," he went on, very smoothly. "So, he is framed. But he is a friend of yours; perhaps you confided in him. So—poor, poor Simon. And—poor Toff!"

He spread that hand again, palm downwards, and kept the gun absolutely still and menacing in his other hand.

"It is a great pity, Rollison. I could have finished this task and gone away, and met you again without you suspecting the truth. You could have lived. Now you will have to go, like the others. Just one little touch of a switch. You—the girls—Raoul, of course, Raoul is down there, I think—and of course, Morency. Simon Leclair, also. Everyone who knows or might know me as Rambeau. You think I am ruthless?"

"Ruthless," murmured the Toff, "is just one word."

"It is good enough," said Rambeau. "But of course I am ruthless; one gets nowhere in this world without that. When I was just an honest man, producing night-club shows, what did I get? Pretty, empty-headed girls with their tantrums, imbeciles who got drunk on champagne and had to be thrown out of the *boites de nuit*, and worry, worry, worry. Never enough money. So, what did I do? I persuaded one of the pretty girls, one who was not a fool, to work on a wealthy old man. She won a fortune from him. Did he report her to the police? Of course not; he was afraid that his wife would find out. So, it all began."

Rollison said slowly: "All right, Rambeau. I can guess what happened next, and how it grew. I can understand why you'll have to kill me, too. But the girls——"

"Those who are hidden here could send me to prison for life, and could ruin all I have done. They were to have been on the way to Algiers soon—some also for the Far East, some for South America. But now——" Rambeau shrugged, and the gun moved, but it did not give the Toff any chance to leap. "It is necessary to wish them all a sad farewell, my friend. I have never killed for the sake of it, but this is necessary. My men have been careless enough to kill, but——"

"Did Violette know your real name?" Rollison asked.

"No, Toff. But one glimpse of me as Rambeau, and she would have known; so she would always be a danger. You have a soft spot for Violette?"

"Don't kill her," Rollison said quietly. "Don't kill any of them."

"Oh, there are plenty of other attractive girls," Rambeau said carelessly. "The sad part is that there is only one Toff. Go down those stairs, please, backwards. I shall cover you all the time. I shall shoot if you show any sign of trying to attack me." He stopped smiling. "At once, please."

The Toff said softly: "No, Chicot. If you kill me, you'll kill me up here. Then the police will come, and the hunt will be up. It doesn't matter what you do, you're finished. Better not have any more murders on your conscience."

Chicot said: "But I have no conscience. If you do not go down those stairs, I shall shoot you where it will cause you a lot of pain." The muzzle of the gun altered its direction, pointing towards Rollison's stomach. "I can satisfy the police. Don't make me hurt you; do what I say."

The Toff stood absolutely still.

There might be a chance, but it was slim; so slim that he did not think that he had a chance to live. There was no real hope for him, but there might be hope for the girls. If he could keep Rambeau away from the switch just long enough for the police to arrive.

So he began to smile.

He saw the puzzlement creep into Rambeau's eyes. He knew that Rambeau felt absolutely sure of himself, but yet could not understand this. He placed the first two fingers of his right hand into his mouth, and kept his left hand raised.

He pulled down his lower lip——

He let forth a whistle, so loud, so piercing, that it made Rambeau wince, and shook him off his guard.

Rollison whistled again.

The sound would travel out of this room, through the garden, over the jetty and the sea, and to the waiting police. They would come racing.

As the second whistle came, Rollison swung round and leapt for the hole in the floor. He heard a shout, then the snap of a shot from Rambeau's gun. He felt a sharp, stabbing pain of a bullet in his side, just below the ribs. He reached the top of the steps, gritting his teeth and preparing to jump. If he knew how to close that hatch from below he might yet have a chance.

A shot roared.

Another came, and he felt nothing.

He couldn't jump, the pain in his side was too great. He felt the warmth of his own blood as it oozed out. He expected another bullet in the back or in the head, but didn't feel it. He started down the stairs, then heard another shot, then two more in quick succession, and realised what he hadn't known before.

The shots were coming from different guns, *and were not at him*.

He was half-way down the steps. He turned, slowly, as pain streaked through his side. He saw Rambeau collapsing, the gun dropping from his hand. In the doorway, water dripping from his body, which was naked but for a pair of blue swimming-trunks, was Panneraude, who held a smoking gun in his right hand.

Out in the dark night, police whistles were shrilling and men were shouting.

"Two men could come here, unheard, if one could do so," declared Panneraude, and his teeth flashed in a delighted smile. "I heard all, my friend, and——"

Rollison hardly heard anything that he said. He saw the change in the Frenchman's expression. Panneraude stopped talking, and jumped towards him. Rollison felt wicked pain. Panneraude seemed to be going round and round. Rambeau was still and silent on the floor, and yet also seemed to be moving. The steps were whirling. The ceiling, the satyrs, Morency, everything was going round and round.

Rollison fell off the steps, losing his balance as unconsciousness swept over him.

He did not know what followed.

He was not there when the girls were brought from the *salon* beneath the cliffs; or when Raoul was brought out, with two other men, by the police; or when Simon Leclair was found, locked in a small room.

Nor was he there when the detonator was taken to pieces and the charge which would have killed a dozen or more people was made harmless.

Instead, he was in hospital.

.   .   .   .   .

"The wound, is it serious?" Simon Leclair demanded. He was looking at Panneraude, hands clenched as if he would strike the policeman. "Answer at once: is it serious?"

Violette was staring tensely, too.

Panneraude had just put down the telephone, after talking to the hospital.

"No," he said, "it is not serious. In a week, or two at the most, he will be walking again. It will be longer than that before he can swim so much or race about, but even that one must rest sometimes." He chuckled. "Now, please, we have work to do, inquiries to make. Understand, the police are not ogres." He looked round at the little statuettes, and shuddered. "And not devils. Much that has been done has been under threat from Rambeau, who called himself Chicot. That applies to you, Mam'selle Monet, and to the other young ladies. I do not think you have great cause to worry."

Violette did not say a word.

Simon Leclair put a hand on her shoulder.

.   .   .   .   .

In London, at Rollison's Mayfair flat, Jolly put down the telephone after a call had come through from Nice. He was smiling, and his brown eyes glowed. He did not know everything, but he knew a great deal. The important thing was that Rollison would be back before long. Perhaps one day he

would meet his match, and lose and die; but not this time,
thank God; not yet.

.   .   .   .   .

Rollison sat up in bed, and stared out of his window over
the deep blue sea. He saw a small white sailing-yacht steal-
ing gently out of sight, and then a motor launch which might
have been the *Maria* or the *Nuit Verte*. He heard the odd
sounds of the street and the beach, and then a tap at the
door.

"Come in," he called.

It was ten days since he had been shot. He felt lazy. His
side was stiff, and the wound had been rather worse than the
doctors had at first thought. It was all very trying. But
when he saw the tow-like red hair of Simon Leclair, he
grinned. The hair, surrounding the bald patch, arrived first.
Simon advanced into the room behind it, bent almost
double, and then looked up and gave that inimitable wink.

"Stand up," said Rollison; "you've won your applause,
and I've laughed."

"Laughter," announced Simon, "feeds the gods. But
friend!" He struck an attitude, opening his mouth wide,
raising his hands, long fingers poking towards the ceiling.
"You have lost the handsome tan, you are so pale. What is
needed for you is the sunny south coast of old England, no?"

"I am as patriotic as the next man," said Rollison, "but
no."

"So." Simon sat down. He drew up his bony knees and let
his long chin rest upon them. "You know everything?" he
inquired.

"Nearly everything," admitted Rollison modestly. "You
tell me the rest."

Simon said soberly: "I have made the inquiries of policeman Panneraude, who is not bad for a policeman, and
Violette and"—he shrugged his shoulders and that seemed to
shrug his knees and his chin. "*Les* girls. Nothing will be

done with them, friend Toff. They acted under the pressure, wasn't it? The police decide, no cases. Plenty of money is found at the Villa, and will be refunded to the poor old men who were made the fools of. I am tempted to declare," said Simon, "that they were served the rights."

Rollison neither agreed nor disagreed with this sentiment or grammar.

"So Violette returns to the fond papa. She is," declared Simon, "a much nicer girl than I believed at first. Just the mistakes, that is all. I 'ope she finds a nice man and he marries her. You," he added, opening one eye very wide, "do not consider marriage. Yes?"

"No."

"It is Fifi," declared Simon. "Matchmaker the incorrectible."

Rollison allowed that to pass, also.

"I was a prisoner, without hope. Thank you," added Simon simply, "for the rescue."

"Thank Violette," murmured Rollison.

"A little Violette, a big Toff." Simon hugged himself tightly. "More things? Gérard is killed in my apartment to make it look like I kill him. Arsenic is planted to make it look I kill you. I am the scrapegoat. A peculiar thing comes next," went on Simon, and wrinkled his nose. "Two of those bad men they employ kill Gérard but leave Violette, because Chicot wants her alive. So, Violette lives to fight another day. I now decide," declared Simon, "that I like that girl very much."

"Don't like her too much," advised the Toff. "Fifi might not approve."

"Oh, one thing is one thing, the other the other," said Simon, with fine exactitude. He waved one hand, dismissing such problems. "Next, please, is the statement made by the Arabs about the poor little maid, Suzanne. The brown boys come to search your room, she finds them, she is going to run for help. So. Very wicked men, all these," Simon declared, and gave the convulsive shrug again. "Like Rambeau. He is the son of the first Chicot, you understand, a bad one. It began because of de Vignolles being a *roué*. Chicot, who loved his sister, had the hatred for rich people, and enjoys to make all of them suffer.

"Right?"

"Grammatically, yes."

"My English improves all the days," boasted Simon proudly. "Some other things. The man Gaston, that beggar who you employ, he is killed. That was Sautot."

"So that was Sautot," echoed Rollison slowly. "Gaston had the photograph of a little girl in his pocket. I would like to find her, and——"

"She is found," Simon said simply. "His child, yes, whom he placed with a poor family, and for whom he paid all he could. But you need not worry, friend. Fifi and I, we have no children. This child is a nice one. So——"

"That's fine," said Rollison. "That's wonderful. There can't be very much more."

"Some little bits, and I will tell you for your blushes," declared Simon. "How scared they are of you! They tell de Vignolles to find out what you know, and he is a failure. You go to the Villa, and Morency makes a big effort to placate you —he shows you that Daphne Myall is alive, does he not?"

"Ah, Daphne. How is——"

"Fine, fine!" announced Simon brightly. "With her mama and papa, here in Nice, one day to be so happy again. So now we know the lots," he added smugly. "Any questions?"

Rollison eased his position a little. The room was shaded, but it was very warm; and another white sail passed before his eyes. He was getting tired.

"Do you know why they decided to kill me?"

"Oh, they were frightened," Simon told him, firmly. "No more. So droll, was it not?"

Droll was a word.

Simon didn't know the truth; and Jolly need never know and feel any sense of guilt.

The Toff began to smile.

"Raoul always will be Raoul," said Simon abruptly, "until they take off his head. But his wife, poor Madeleine, is free to mourn her brother and to hate her husband. But she is alive, and she is beautiful—like all of them," the clown added, with unexpected tenderness, "and I wish them all the wells."

He moved, uncoiling himself, then, standing at his full height and looking down with his head on one side:

"Pal," he announced, "you are tired. I go. In the morning, Violette will come to see you. She is grateful to the lunatic Englishman. Also Fifi. Also Panneraude. You have," he announced severely, "many more responsibilities now, Toff. You have so many more friends."

THE END